The goon with the eyebrow jewelry loomed in front of Gaia, grinning maniacally. He, too, had a knife—a crude, blunt hunting blade.

"I knew you would be back," he said in his high, frenzied pitch.

"Is that so?" Gaia responded.

"Yeah. God told me." He lunged toward her, arms flailing wildly.

"Oh, please." What was this? A fight or a sermon? She'd had her fill of religious-sounding street trash.

And with a high, exhilarating kick, she sent him flying backwards into one of his buddies. Their heads collided, knocking them senseless.

How could she have ever found this daunting? She was like a racehorse that had been stabled for far too long. Her limbs and muscles practically sang with pleasure. This was what she was meant to do. She knew it with every hormonally charged molecule in her being.

Don't miss any books in this thrilling series:

FEARLESS™

Available from SIMON PULSE

FEARLESS™

FAKE

FRANCINE PASCAL

SIMON PULSE
New York   London   Toronto   Sydney

This book is a work of fiction. Any references to historical events, real people, or real locales are used fictitiously. Other names, characters, places, and incidents are the product of the author's imagination, and any resemblance to actual events or locales or persons, living or dead, is entirely coincidental.

First Simon Pulse edition July 2004

Copyright © 2004 by Francine Pascal

Cover copyright © 2004 by 17th Street Productions, an Alloy company.

SIMON PULSE
An imprint of Simon & Schuster Children's Publishing Division
1230 Avenue of the Americas, New York, NY 10020

 Produced by 17th Street Productions,
an Alloy company
151 West 26th Street
New York, NY 10001

All rights reserved, including the right of reproduction in whole or in part in any form.
For information address 17th Street Productions, 151 West 26th Street, New York, NY 10001.

Fearless™ is a trademark of Francine Pascal.

Printed in the United States of America
10 9 8 7 6 5 4 3 2 1

Library of Congress Control Number: 2004100272
ISBN: 0-689-86917-7

To Jean Yves Santini

It always used to amaze me how many words there were to describe a fear state. I once looked it up in the thesaurus and there were about a kajillion. *Terrified, worried, frightened, anxious, horrified, panicked, fretful, scared, petrified, apprehensive. . .* Apparently fear is to English what ice is to Inuit.

And that doesn't even take into account the "baseless" fears. Those "bad feelings" people refer to that tell them when to run and hide. I read about this stuff in the newspapers. Some businessman feels prickles on the back of his neck and for no reason other than a vague fear debarks a plane that later crashes. A married couple feels strangely uneasy while looking at what is otherwise their dream house and decide not to buy it— then later find out it's become the site of a mass murder. Even animals seem able to sense when bad stuff is coming.

The only time I felt something slightly akin to this was when I was four. It wasn't fear at all, more like a hollow outline of it—the difference between early Atari and Xbox. A muddled sense that things were NOT RIGHT.

When I was four, my mom became pregnant. Over the months I'd watched her stomach bulge out like a very slow-filling balloon. I remember her flushed cheeks and faraway looks. She was so excited about the new baby. Dad too. Me? I was indifferent. Based on my limited experience with babies, I couldn't logically understand why my parents were giddy about getting a loud, stinky creature who couldn't do anything.

Eventually the big day came. Mom went off to the hospital with that eager blush on her cheeks, kissing me before waddling out the door. Then Dad kissed me and promised they'd be back soon with the baby. Only they didn't come back soon. I overheard my babysitter, old Mrs. Jorgensen (who always smelled like cat food), talking to my dad on the phone. She had her back to me and was mumbling quietly into the receiver, but I managed to catch the words *tests* and *lack of oxygen*. When she hung up, she tried to act like nothing was wrong, but I'd learned to read people by that time. Adults always try to keep bad news from children in order not to scare them. Only I couldn't be scared. And I knew a lousy acting job when I saw it.

So I waited. Slowly the day fell into shadows, then darkened completely. Then that evening my dad finally came home. His face was pearly pale and he told me the baby wasn't coming home after all—there had been a mix-up and the baby had gone to heaven instead. He also said that Mom was going to have to stay longer in the hospital and maybe I could go see her in a couple of days.

Of course, little did I know that my brother *did* survive the birth. An underground organization kidnapped him for themselves, hoping he would also possess fearlessness—or at least the secrets to it. Years later I would get nabbed by the same group of thugs and thrown in a mental institution. There I would meet a beautiful, sweet, completely innocent boy known only as D. My brother. My flesh and blood.

The day of D.'s birth, the day of not-right feelings, was the start of a horrific pattern in my life: people I love being taken from me one way or another, all because of my fearlessness. And now that I have fear, in spite of the fact that I seem to be existing in a state of constant anxiety, there is one slight comfort. Maybe now that I'm no longer fearless, the pattern will stop. Maybe people will stop messing with those I love.

Looking back on the variety pack of tragedies in my life has never been fun, but it's practically unbearable now. Reliving these moments physically grips me in a vise of grief and panic, almost as if it's happening again. . . . My mom lying in bed after losing the baby—her stomach flat and empty, her face sickly white, almost transparent with grief. My dad staring into space for hours at a time, hardly noticing me. And that not-right feeling I had—that creeping disorientation—that underscored my sadness.

Now that I look back, I suddenly see that feeling for what it truly was—one of those fear premonitions, a warning of the next awful tragedy in store for me. A time when Mom would never come back.

So, maybe there's more to fear than I originally thought. Call it instinct, ESP, good or bad vibes—whatever. Maybe fear actually tunes people in to the cosmos and lets them see what's coming to pass.

Bad feelings? I've got loads of them. And right now they're telling me awful things are on the way.

His eyes were
like a pair of
floodlights—
bright, **bitch—**
steady, **slapped**
mesmerizing.
She could feel **by**
herself **reality**
wilting
beneath
them. . . .

LOKI STOOD BEFORE HIS EIGHTEENTH- story window, staring out at the night sky. The nearby buildings were cast in a palette of varying grays, like the set of a Japanese monster movie. Beyond them the city's lights stretched out toward the horizon, like tiny holes in the threadbare darkness.

She was out there somewhere. His Gaia. Possibly behind one of those pricks of light. Maybe even fighting for her life.

Normally he wouldn't worry. She was strong, his girl. A modern Valkyrie. He had no doubt she could overpower or outmaneuver anything the city threw at her. But this was different. Right now she was in the hands of someone he didn't trust—someone who also realized what invaluable gems she carried in her genetic code. Skyler Rodke.

Loki turned his back to the window and snatched his alphanumeric pager off the waistband of his slacks. He held it up, letting the city lights bounce off the sleek black display screen. Still no messages. He set the pager down on a nearby console and pulled a fifty-cent piece from his left pocket. He turned the coin over and over in his hands, feeling the metal grow warm in his grasp.

He could send out an alert, rally all of his operatives in the search for Gaia. But that would be rash. It was quite possible one of them had turned on him, passing along vital secrets to this competitor. Ever since his return, it had been difficult to know his men's loyalties. All those weeks he'd lain useless in a hospital bed, they had been cut off and left to fend for themselves—body parts without a brain. He could almost understand it if one of them had latched on, leechlike, to another willing leader.

Patience, he thought as he repocketed his coin and walked over to the teak-and-leather bar on the opposite side of the room. He would not send out an APB. Frustrating as this was, it would be far better to wait than risk informing his nemesis of his panicked state.

Plus he had the boy.

It wasn't the same. Jake Montone was no operative. He had no subtlety. And he lacked the necessary ability to surgically sever all emotional ties and simply follow orders. The boy complicated things, but he did have one advantage that a whole team of trained professionals, including Loki himself, did not have: Gaia, for some reason, trusted the boy.

And he's proving easy to mold, Loki admitted generously, filling a highball glass halfway with ice cubes and drenching them in amber-colored scotch. *He's green but enthusiastic—eager to be Gaia's knight in shining armor.*

As long as he was a willing servant and Gaia let him near her, Loki would continue to use the boy. Jake wasn't much of a secret weapon in a crisis such as this. But then, given the right circumstances, even a pawn could defeat a king.

THE SCREEN FADED TO BLACK. THE

Dust Bunny from Hell

theme music swelled, filling the apartment with its mournful melody. Gaia lay across the orange plaid couch, her head in Skyler's lap. The turquoise-and-navy Columbia University blanket he had tossed over her was making her arm itch, but she didn't scratch. She could feel Skyler stretch his arms—first up, then out—but she remained immobile, her eyes transfixed upon the words scrolling up the thirty-six-inch television screen. She was motionless yet tense, like a spring-loaded trap, powerless to untangle her mind from the *Godfather* universe.

Her gut felt bunched and her heart seemed to be throbbing in pain instead of simply beating. The whole time she was watching the film, an awful dread had crept over her. She felt vulnerable and exposed, as if a cold-blooded gunman might jump out from behind the couch at any moment.

And knowing her life, it could happen.

Skyler placed his hand on her shoulder and shook it gently. "You awake?" he murmured.

"Mm-hmm," she replied. She sat up slowly, hugging her knees to her chest.

"So, you want to watch something else?" Skyler asked, hitting the power button on the remote. The music stopped suddenly. Now all Gaia could hear was the thudding of her heartbeat and the nasal whine of her breathing.

She shook her head.

"Okay. So what do you want to do?"

What did she want to do?

The world of mafiosi was gradually fading as her own reality took back color and form. Skyler's apartment was all foreign shadows. She could make out the familiar lump of her backpack, still streaked with mud from her tussle with the IV heads. Her jacket lay across a nearby chair. It looked rumpled and neglected, a forlorn shape among all the blocky masculine furniture.

A siren sounded nearby, screeching louder and then dopplering away. Gaia drew her legs tighter against her chest. Her world wasn't any better than the one in the movie. In fact, it was worse. Hers was darker, more chaotic. Existing in it made her feel worn out and defeated— bitch-slapped by reality. Right now all she wanted was to curl up and ignore everything forever.

"Gaia?" Skyler prompted.

"I think I need to go," she said, pushing off the couch and reaching down for her tennis shoes.

"What?" Skyler sat up straight, his thick brows scrolling together over his nose. "Wait a second. I thought you were staying over. What's wrong?"

Gaia felt a pang of guilt as she tied her shoes. Skyler had been so nice to take her in after the fight. It wasn't his fault she'd turned into a big, depressing lump. But she wouldn't be any fun if she stayed around. A college guy like Skyler had better things to do than babysit a scared high school girl. "I'm sorry. I just don't feel up for much," she said, rising to her feet. "Where's my phone? Can I have it back?"

He smiled crookedly. "No."

"Ha ha. Very funny," she said weakly. "Now hand it over, please."

"Uh-uh." He settled back against the couch cushions and put his hands behind his head. "Look, you're all worked up again, I can tell. And the whole point of you coming over here tonight was to relax, right?"

"Yeah, but—"

"No. No arguments. I'm not going to let you leave until I've accomplished my mission."

Gaia stared at him. His eyes were like a pair of floodlights—bright, steady, mesmerizing. She could feel herself wilting beneath them until finally she sank back onto the couch beside him.

He was right. It was late. Besides, after the fight and the movie she was too weirded out to face the city beyond the doors just yet.

"Okay," she said, kicking her shoes back off. "But I'm warning you, I'm not going to be any fun."

"Fine. No fun allowed." He sat back and crossed his arms over his chest, his face a mask of seriousness. She could tell he was trying to make her laugh, but she was way too depressed for it to work. Still, she managed a feeble smile to be polite.

"Here." He turned the TV back on and handed her the remote. "Now I want you to know I don't do this for just anyone. Relinquishing channel surf power is about the highest honor I can give you."

"Thanks." She settled back and began pressing the channel button, assessing each image as it passed. A medical drama? No. Men in suits talking about war? No. Late-night hosts joking about war? No. A live report from a ten-alarm fire in the Midwest? Cartoon characters braiding each other's intestines? No. No. No.

Gaia switched off the power, feeling more distressed than ever. Two hundred channels and all of it unsettling. Why had she never noticed how terrible TV was?

"Don't feel like watching anything?" Skyler asked. His eyes were wide and wary, as if he feared any moment she might start bouncing around his apartment like a crazed Looney Tunes character. And what made it worse was she couldn't promise she wouldn't.

"Not really," she said, handing him back the remote. "If you don't mind, I think I'll just go lie down." She stood and stretched out her arms for effect.

Actually she wasn't sleepy, but she did feel wrung out, like a `ragged dishrag` that had scrubbed too many pots. She could almost hear the commercial: *Gaia Moore, human SOS pad—use her to scour scum off the city streets, then discard her in the nearest ditch!*

"No problem. I'm sure you're tired." He stood and placed a steady hand on her shoulder. "You've been through a lot."

Gaia closed her throat tightly and stared down at her threadbare athletic socks. "Thanks," she mumbled, pondering the hole over her right big toe. She didn't want to meet his eyes. As it was, his consoling touch had sent a fresh fountain of self-pity surging through her. Any more niceness and she'd be all blubber.

"Here," he said steering her toward the bedroom. "Let me show you the—"

"No," she interrupted, sliding out from under his hand. She didn't want him to come with her. She was too close to breaking down, too close to revealing how raw and weak she really was. She might not be fearless anymore, but she still had that loner instinct against letting people see her vulnerable. And Skyler had already seen too much.

"Don't worry. I'll be okay," she said, lifting her head

but not quite meeting Skyler's gaze. "Thanks for everything. Good night."

She trudged around the corner to the darkened bedroom. The light from the living area revealed a king-size bed, a workout bench, and a tall oak dresser covered with gadgets and papers. Leaving her clothes on, Gaia slipped under the thick denim comforter and curled into a fetal position.

But she couldn't sleep. She couldn't relax or disconnect her mind. With nothing to see or hear, her thoughts veered inward, each one slowly deforming into a paralyzing fear. She thought of her dad, then wondered where he was, then panicked that he might be in danger. She thought of Ed, then pictured him palling around with Kai, then fell into an agonizing nostalgia for him. She thought of her brother, D., then almost suffocated on her bitterness toward those who'd snatched him away. *Dad? Ed? Sam? Jake?* Everything warped grotesquely. Everything led to misery.

And amid all the disturbing thoughts was another: vague dread. It was as if she could feel the evil of the city seeping in through the cracks in the building, surrounding her, collecting under the bed like a gigantic dust bunny from hell. Having grown up fearless, she'd never entertained childlike terrors of monsters under the bed or getting sucked down the bathtub drain. But now, with the creeping panic overtaking her mind, she could understand such fears.

Lying there, curled up and alone in a chilly bedroom, it seemed quite possible—even likely—that this amorphous wickedness could reach up from beneath the bed, encircle her with its cold, clammy arms, and pull her down, down into a choking black abyss. If she stayed still and silent, maybe it wouldn't notice her. Maybe it would just go away.

Gaia's hand gripped the top of the mattress, her breath coming in short, ragged gasps. How did people do this? How did they live with their fears? The real world was such a nightmare—she knew it before, but now she could *feel* it. Everywhere there was danger, hatred, malice. She could see why people turned to drugs and alcohol or formed gangs and mafias—the better to fight corruption with corruption.

But what did she have? How could she cope? Was there absolutely nothing that could give her comfort and let her sleep at night? She closed her eyes and performed a quick mental Google search until she finally hit upon a face. . . the most beautiful face in the world. Her mother. That's what she wanted right now. Her mom's lilting voice and soft, cool touch. Only. . . she couldn't have that. She could never have that again.

Hot tears gathered behind her closed lids and a jagged lump rose in her throat. Just then Gaia heard a shuffling sound and felt the bed quake slightly. A hand touched her forehead. *Mom?* No. It was Skyler. She felt him slide under the covers and contour his body around hers, his chest against her back, his knees folding into the angle of her legs. He was still dressed. She debated opening her eyes and looking at him, but she continued to feign sleep, wondering where this was leading.

Then suddenly she felt a warm weight on her. Skyler's left arm circled around her middle, his elbow nestled in the crook between her hip and rib cage. Gaia felt strangely reassured by the gesture. It was as if his arm was mooring her down, preventing her from spiraling off into the nightmare void. Gradually her panic subsided and her thoughts became less and less tormenting, until they took on the fuzzy, garbled quality of presleep.

Gaia reached up and placed her right hand on Skyler's forearm before finally, peacefully drifting off.

A SMATTERING OF RAINDROPS SMEARED

the ink on the battered computer printout in Jake's hand. *Great,* he thought. *Just what I need.*

He'd already wasted two vital hours walking Broadway and Amsterdam, checking each of the Columbia University dorms for one Skyler Rodke—rich pretty

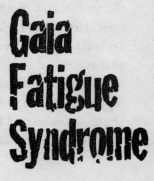

Gaia Fatigue Syndrome

boy and possible kidnapper. Too bad he hadn't hit the 114th Street student housing first. Just his luck to find the guy in the last-possible place.

He headed down the block, checking the addresses against the list in his hand. Eventually he stopped and stared at a somber redbrick building. *This is the last one,* he thought, crumpling up the paper and tossing it into a nearby wrought iron trash can. *Skyler has to be here.*

Skyler Rodke. Even his name sounded like a soap opera scandal waiting to happen. Jake's fingers opened and closed into fists, eager for the chance to collide with Skyler's salon-product-enhanced skin and reshape his Prince William nose.

"Easy," Jake whispered to himself, digging the blunt points of his right knuckles against his left palm. He had to be cool about this. He was there as an operative, not a boyfriend. Going Jet Li on the guy would only screw up the mission.

He could only hope Rodke picked a fight first.

He had this friend once, a karate buddy. The guy dropped out of classes at the dojo because he came down with some sort of chronic fatigue virus. He said it was a disease he would never get rid of. It just dawdled around in his system, waiting for his body to get the slightest bit weak. Then it would spring into action, making his joints ache and his muscles floppy, until the guy just had to go to bed for a couple of days or weeks, waiting for it to pass.

At the time Jake didn't buy it. It sounded like some cockamamie cover story. The guy was probably too lazy or chicken to put in the required effort for black belt status and just didn't want to face the truth.

Now Jake believed him. He too felt like he was also carrying around a pernicious little germ that liked to kick him when he was down. He was infected with Gaia Moore. And it wasn't a onetime thing either. He was a Gaia carrier, a victim of `Gaia fatigue syndrome`.

Once Gaia had come into his life, nothing had been the same. It was as if some small scrap of her was inhabiting his body, had set up shop, and rewritten his chemical code. His priorities did a complete Chinese fire drill, recataloging themselves into a basic, fixed list: Gaia, Gaia, eat, sleep, Gaia.

It wasn't just that he was in love with her. That was way too crude a term. This was more sweeping and uncompromising, more. . . diseaselike. At times he felt giddy and feverish with devotion to her. Other times he felt pulled down by her, wearied by all the turmoil in her life that was now seeping into his own. Lately she'd even started acting clingy and needy—not at all like the headstrong, independent girl he fell in love with.

But even that wouldn't push him away. There was no escaping it, no purging Gaia from his system. She was part of him now. To cut her out, he'd have to destroy himself. Besides, he didn't want to be free of her. He loved the messy, aching, maddening ride that was Gaia. He'd never felt more alive in his entire life. Gaia had given him a purpose, a calling, a brand-new realm to exist in. He couldn't help feeling that everything that had ever happened to him had led him to this—to her.

If only something would lead him to her now.

A group of students came scurrying up the sidewalk, holding bags and jackets over their heads to protect against the rain. Jake fell into step behind them, matching their hurried pace. By now he knew the drill. He followed them up the concrete steps underneath the arched stone entrance. One of the girls at the head of the group pulled out her key card and swiped it through a black box on the exterior wall. With an irritable buzz, the front door opened and the group filed into the yellow-lighted lobby.

Jake grinned. No one gave him a passing glance as they shook water off their jackets and headed toward the elevators. He was proud he'd developed this little infiltration system on his own. It was so much easier than shouting through the outside intercom, as he'd had to do at the first couple of dorms. Plus it made him feel like a real agent—using his wits, blending in with the crowd.

At the other side of the foyer, a man in a security guard's uniform was sitting behind a gray laminate counter. He barely glanced up as Jake approached.

"Can I help you?" the guard asked.

"Yes," Jake said, leaning against the counter. "I'm looking for a girl."

The man frowned.

Great, Jake. Brilliant opening. Now he thinks you're the world's lamest playboy. "I mean. . . I'm looking for a *particular* girl—a friend of mine," he tried again. He took a breath and launched into his rehearsed explanation. "You see, there's been an emergency in her family and I need to find her, but she isn't answering her cell phone. All I know is that she's out with a Columbia student named Skyler Rodke. Would he happened to be listed at this dorm?"

The guard nodded slightly for a few seconds, as if he needed extra time to process the information. Then he sighed and rubbed his eyes. "Hang on. Let me check the registry."

Jake drummed his fingertips against the gray laminate as the guard sluggishly typed commands into the computer. *Come on, come on. All sorts of things could be happening to Gaia.* He resisted the urge to leap over the counter, shove the guard out of the way, and search the log himself.

Eventually the man pushed back his chair and turned toward Jake. "Sorry. There's no one by that name listed."

"What?" Jake leaned forward and gaped at the monitor. "No way!"

Jake realized he must have been screaming, because

a group of students paused in their conversation to stare at him. The guard held up a warning hand. "Back away from the computer, sir," he said with sudden authority.

"I'm sorry," Jake said, lowering his voice. "It's just. . . I've got to find her, and I've already tried all the other dorms. Are you sure you got the name right? Rodke? *R-o-d-k-e?*"

"I'm positive," the man replied. "There's no Rodke and no Skyler anything listed. Now if you'll excuse me," he added with a nod toward the exit, "I have some work to do."

Jake took a few aimless steps away from the desk, shaking his head in disbelief. This couldn't be happening. He'd tried everywhere. All that work, all that effort, and he was no closer to finding Gaia than he had been three hours ago.

What now? What the hell was he going to tell Oliver?

"Excuse me?"

Jake looked up. A pretty redhead with stick-straight Avril Lavigne hair was leaning toward him somewhat cautiously.

"I couldn't help overhearing," she said, meeting his bewildered gaze. "Are you looking for Skyler Rodke?"

"Yes!" Jake rounded on her. "Do you know him? Do you know where he is?"

The girl swayed backward slightly, her eyes widening in alarm. "I. . . I know who he is, but I don't know him. He goes to Columbia, but he lives off campus."

Off campus? The thought washed through Jake's mind, scrubbing it clear. *Of course! Why didn't I realize that before? A guy like Skyler would have his own place. He'd never stoop as low as dorm life.*

"Where? Where does he live?" His restlessness was back, tightening his fists and amplifying his voice.

The girl kept her gaze on him but turned her body away, clearly sorry she'd ever approached him. "I don't know. I've just heard he has a fancy apartment somewhere. It's just talk. You know? People talk about him."

"Right," Jake said, nodding distractedly. Then he placed his palms together in a prayerlike gesture. "Thank you! You saved me!"

"No problem," the girl muttered before hurrying back to her friends by the elevator.

Jake bounded back to the front counter. "Excuse me?" he asked the guard. "Could I borrow your white pages?"

The man gave a frustrated huff and slid the giant book toward Jake, who immediately began leafing through it.

"Roddenberry. . . Roddick. . . Roditi. . . ," he mumbled as his finger slid slowly down the page. "Yes! Rodke." There was a John out in Queens, a Sarah with a Chelsea exchange, and then a bunch of "Rodkey" spellings. No Skyler. Not even a half-anonymous S. Rodke with a Manhattan listing. Nothing.

Jake slammed the book shut and returned it to the

guard with a mumbled "thanks." Then he walked back out the front door into the rain.

Gaia was someplace close, he could feel it. But he had no idea how to get to her. He was like a rat in a maze of dead ends, and a fragrant block of cheese was sitting just beyond the walls.

Gaia, please, he urged silently, straining to seek out her mind through the walls of the nearby buildings. *Please just answer my messages. Call me. Before it's too late.*

This probably never happens to real undercover operatives. Or at least it shouldn't—not to the good ones, anyway.

I know how it's supposed to unfold. I grew up watching the spy serials. All those stories of daring rescue and intrigue, where the hero saves the world in a thousand-dollar suit. I just knew that could be me someday, disarming the bad guys and knocking them senseless. Then carrying the hot blond to safety only seconds before a bomb exploded in a supernova of fire and smoke. Obviously I'm not cut out for this after all, since I seem to have all the spy instincts of a garden slug.

Oliver is counting on me to find Gaia. Gaia needs me. And I'm letting them down.

I never realized just how freaking hard this spy stuff is. Where are the scared informants whispering vital information to me from out of the shadows?

Where are the clues? A book bag or scuffed tennis shoe or some other Gaia-like debris pointing the way to her hideaway? I could use a cryptic SOS message on my answering machine or a taunting riddle from the baddies—anything to use as a starting place in this whole screwed-up cat-and-mouse game.

James Bond never made mistakes. He never burst into someone's lair only to find a group of women playing mah-jongg—"Very sorry. Pardon me. Please carry on"—or nabbed an innocent bystander or aimlessly wandered the city streets for hours.

And Oliver would never be stuck in neutral like this. He'd have located Gaia in under ten minutes. I know he wants me to do it because Gaia's still freaked into thinking he's Loki again, but obviously I don't deserve his faith in me.

So I'll make a deal with the cosmos. Forget my earlier dreams. I don't need to be a big hero.

I'll just settle for this: to
find Gaia in one piece before
anything awful happens. The rest
you can take from there.

John
continued to
pelt her
with bricks,
laughing **crazed**
as if he
were **stare**
playing a
two-dollar
carnival
game.

GAIA WOKE UP TO THE EARTHY, smoky smell of fresh coffee being brewed. The rectangle of glass between the curtains revealed putty-colored clouds hanging over the nearby buildings, the view oddly distorted by the film of grimy rainwater on the window.

She took a deep breath and stretched her arms up as high as they could go without rapping against the mahogany headboard. Then she rolled over.

The bed was still warm where Skyler had lain next to her. Even her waist still felt warm and weighty, the ghost of his arm anchoring her down to the bed all night. Gaia smiled. She could hear him in the kitchen, singing something. A Coldplay song. *God give me style and give me grace. . . .* She closed her eyes and followed the melody, the clattering sounds of cups, and the whoosh of cars passing on the slick streets below.

After a minute she felt the bed shimmy. Skyler crept over the mattress and lay down beside her, his arm returning to its spot across her belly.

"Good morning," he sang into her ear. "How did you sleep?"

She opened her eyes. "Good," she said with a grin.

"I'm glad." He smiled his toothy, glow-in-the-dark smile. "See? I knew it. All you needed was to take a break from it all and relax. Do you feel better?"

"Yeah. Just. . . tired."

"You should go back to sleep," he said, patting the curve of her waist before pulling his arm away.

Gaia reflexively put her own arm in the spot he vacated. She didn't want to tell him that she wasn't sleepy. Instead she was tired in that posttrauma kind of way—the collapsing sense of relief you feel after a great pressure had been lifted. But he'd been right about one thing. Staying over had helped. She felt two hundred percent better than she had the night before. It was just so nice and simple being here—just her and Skyler hiding out from the rest of the world.

A new thought occurred to her. "Is your roommate here?" she asked, peeking through the crack in the doorway to the living room beyond.

"Relax. It's just us." He placed his hand on her shoulder and gently pushed her back against the mattress. "Carl left a note. He's gone upstate to visit his parents this weekend."

"Oh," she said, settling back into the bedcovers. She was glad it was just the two of them. Things were perfect—better than they had been in a while. Adding someone else to the mix would only upset the beautiful whatever she had going here.

"I made coffee." Skyler slid out of bed and ran his fingers through his unkempt blond hair. "But you don't have to get up. It rained all last night and it's still drizzling. Good morning to sleep in."

She turned back toward the window. "There'll be rainbows in the puddles," she said distractedly.

"What's that? Rainbows?"

"In the puddles," she finished. She glanced at Skyler and gave a bashful shrug. "It's nothing. Just this thing I used to do when I was a weird little kid."

"What? Tell me." He sat on the edge of the bed, watching her with a bemused expression.

"It's stupid."

He put his hand on her calf, shaking it gently. "Come on. I really want to know."

Gaia raised herself up on her elbows and tilted back her head as if sunning on a virtual beach. She shut her eyes and remembered herself as a knobby-jointed five-year-old. "After it rained at our old house," she began, "I used to love to go out to the nearby road and look at the puddles in the potholes."

"And splash in them?"

"Well, yeah. But I loved the way there would be this ring of color in the center of the puddle, like each one had its own rainbow. I thought it was beautiful. It wasn't until I was a little older that my dad explained how toxic chemicals from the car engines made that design—not rainbows."

Gaia could see her father's face swimming before her, gently reprimanding her for playing in the noxious water. Then her mother, shaking her head and making that disapproving clicking sound, barely hiding her amusement. Before she could descend into grief, Gaia opened her eyes. Skyler was smiling at her.

It was the kindest smile she'd seen in a long time. An adoring smile.

"That's beautiful," he said. "I'm glad you told me that. I want to hear more. I want to know everything about you."

Lukewarm tears—happy or sad, she couldn't tell—collected in the corners of her eyes. It was too late to bully them back into her ducts. Instead she gave an enormous fake yawn and rubbed the renegade drops with the back of her hands.

"You should go back to sleep." Skyler gave her leg another friendly pat and got to his feet. "Maybe later you can tell me more. Right now I'm going to take a quick shower."

"Okay," she said, settling back against the pillows.

"You going to be all right?" he asked, unbuttoning his shirt.

"Yeah."

Gaia hugged a pillow and watched as he slid off his shirt and tossed it into a nearby wicker hamper. His trademark Rodke-smooth skin glimmered in the feeble light. His chest was muscular—but in a rough-cut, choppy way, different from the sloping curves of Jake's strapping build. It was as if Jake had been carefully molded from clay while Skyler had been chiseled out of cool marble.

He met her gaze and grinned. "Get some rest. I'll be in here if you need anything." He stepped into the bathroom and shut the door behind him. Soon she could hear the water come on and Skyler began humming the Coldplay song again.

An intense feeling of gratitude came over her. If it wasn't for Skyler, she'd be waking up in her bare, depressing little room back at Collingwood, spiraling down the big despair drain again. She was glad he'd made her stay. It was like he knew just what she needed. He gave her space, yet he held her all night—as if he somehow understood she needed an anchor.

Not just anyone would take in a wretched, depressing blob of a girl. She wished she could do something to show her thanks, maybe even get him some sort of gift. But what? Like all the Rodkes, Skyler had everything. All he truly needed was water, oxygen, and the regular intake of nutrients.

Wait. That's it. Gaia sat up straight. The guy needed food, right? So why not get him breakfast? She couldn't cook—at least, she shouldn't if she wanted to reward the guy—but she *could* surprise him with a bagel tray.

She hopped out of bed and headed into the living room to find her shoes. Yes. That's exactly what she'd do. She'd go down the street, pick up some bagels, and hopefully be back before he came out of the shower.

Gaia grabbed her jacket and practically skipped

out the door. She couldn't wait. Skyler was going to be *so* surprised.

JAKE TRUDGED UP THE PORCH STEPS

Bad-Girl Facade

of the Collingwood boarding-house and caught a dim reflection of himself in the front window. He could have been cast as a mysterious drifter in a movie. His dark wavy hair looked like a mess of blown wires after being drenched with rain and dried in the breeze. His eyes were slightly sunken, and a crop of whiskers had overtaken the lower half of his face. All he needed was the moth-eaten knit cap and he could have been featured on those home security system flyers that came in the mail: PROTECT YOUR HOME FROM THIS MAN.

He made a halfhearted attempt to tame his hair and then rang the buzzer. He could hear it echo inside the house, followed by the iambic rhythm of someone bounding down the stairs. *Please, please, please let it be Gaia*, he prayed silently.

The door creaked open and a girl's face leaned into the crack. "Oh, hey," she said, now opening the door just enough to reveal the rest of her.

It wasn't Gaia. Zan, Gaia's spacey housemate, leaned lazily against the door frame. She looked out of place. A night creature caught in the light of morning.

Her eyes peered up at him between thick streaks of eyeliner, and her long dirt-blond hair hung in near dreds, spilling over the shoulders of her black Mickey Mouse T-shirt.

"Can I please speak with Gaia?" Jake asked.

"She's not here," Zan replied, a wry smile curling her red, bloodstained-looking lips. "In fact," she added, watching Jake closely, "she hasn't been here all night." She curled her left leg around the doorway, her stockinged foot tracing figure-eight patterns on the porch planks.

So she's still with Skyler. A white-hot rage welled up inside him, but he somehow managed to steady his features. He had been hoping, even praying that Gaia would be here, but deep down, he'd known she wouldn't be. So far it had been his only instinct that proved right.

"Do you know where she is? Did she leave a number?" he asked, wincing at the chime of desperation in his voice.

Zan grinned. Impish sparks glimmered behind her bloodshot eyes. "I don't know anything. But then, sometimes people don't want to be found, right?"

Jake didn't answer. His jaw clenched reflexively.

"But you're welcome to hang out with me." She crossed the threshold onto the porch, her hands toying

34

with the doorknob behind her back. "I know some cool places. And I can get some great stuff." She reached out her foot and slid her toes up his shin. "I could make you forget about Gaia."

"No. Uh, thanks anyway," Jake said, resisting the urge to kick her foot away.

For a split second Zan's sultry bad-girl facade fell away, revealing the face of a pouty child. Even the thick black makeup couldn't hide it. She looked like a doll someone had kicked around and colored on.

Then, as quickly as it appeared, the look was gone. The sullen teenager returned, even more sullen than before. "Whatever," she snapped. "Your loss." She headed back into the house.

"Wait," Jake called.

Zan turned back, a glimmer of anticipation in her eyes.

"If you see Gaia, would you tell her to call me?" he asked. Watching her features harden, he smiled and added, "Please?"

"We'll see." She flashed one last ironic grin and then shut the door in his face.

Jake descended the steps and looked down the awakening street. His worst fears had now been confirmed—Gaia was still gone. Still off frolicking with the King of Face Creams. And he was still left with no leads. His cosmic bargaining didn't seem to be working out.

He took a deep breath of muggy morning air and slowly massaged his temples. His stomach churned with a frothy brew of emotions, made even more bitter by lack of sleep. Could he have brought this on himself? Maybe this was punishment for something terrible he'd done. If only he could remember what it was.

If he ever saw Gaia again. . . No, *when* he saw Gaia again, he would hold her close and promise to listen to her—even her paranoid delusions about Oliver turning evil. He would be the most attentive, least argumentative, best boyfriend on the planet.

That or he'd kick her ass.

POST-RAIN NEW YORK WAS SMELLIER

than usual, but it wasn't without its charms. The foliage looked fresh and dewy. The sidewalks gleamed as if freshly waxed. And the buildings seemed stripped of a layer of grime, their graffiti shining bright and colorful.

Snakelike Tentacles

No rainbows today, though. On a whim Gaia had glanced into a nearby puddle, but all she saw was mud.

She was walking briskly down the street, toward

the corner where she was pretty sure she'd seen a bakery, when all of a sudden she felt something grab at her ankle. Gaia hopped sideways and shook her leg. Glancing down, she realized it was only her shoelaces flapping about her leg.

Jeez, what a spaz, she thought, stepping to the far side of the sidewalk to retie her sneaker. *Will I ever stop freaking at every little thing?*

As she crouched over the slick cement, something white caught her eye. Looking closer, she saw it was a dead baby bird lying in a small pool of rainwater, the fragments of its tawny shell all around it. Gaia felt her despair returning, its cold, snakelike tentacles coiling around her organs, darkening her thoughts.

Poor thing, she thought, staring at the lifeless bird. It was such a tiny, exquisite corpse. She was struck by the detail on each downy feather, the twisted pink twig of a leg.

The storm must have knocked it out of the nearby tree. Little guy hadn't had a chance. For weeks he had been snug and safe in its perfect oval sanctum and then *bam!* All he had gotten to know of the world outside was pain and death.

She understood such suffering. She herself had recently burst out of her fearless cocoon into the real live world. And so far, most of what she'd come to know was agony.

Gaia wiped a tear from the corner of her eye. She

couldn't leave the bird like this, dumped unceremoniously onto a grimy sidewalk. In a way, she felt like this could be her own demise she was glimpsing. It wasn't much of a stretch to imagine herself lying dead in a ditch, with clueless pedestrians flinging cigarette butts and hocking loogeys on her as they passed, too busy to notice or care.

As tenderly as she could, she scooped the frail figure into her hand. He looked so cold and wet and alone. Gaia pulled a wad of Kleenex out of her jacket pocket and carefully wrapped him in it. Then she folded the ends until he was completely shrouded.

Now what? She peered down a nearby alley and saw just what she was looking for. Midway down, next to a large gray Dumpster, lay a spot of fresh earth between broken bits of asphalt. She walked over and dug her fingers into the damp dirt until she'd hollowed out a small grave. Then she laid him inside and covered him up.

Should I say something? she wondered as she pressed the dirt level with the street. After all, it was a funeral—impromptu and slightly ridiculous, but still a funeral.

She rummaged through her mind for something appropriate to say, something philosophical and uplifting.

"Life is hell, isn't it?"

The voice had come from somewhere nearby, a little farther down the alley. Gaia ducked behind the Dumpster and listened. She was quite sure she didn't know the person behind the voice, but there was still something recognizable about its restless, energized tone.

"Make him scream, John. I wanna hear him scream," came another, more keyed-up voice.

Gaia peered through the triangular gap between the Dumpster and the alley wall. They were just a few yards down. Two guys were menacing another who was backed up against the wall. Their jerky movements and the way they were practically panting with excitement were all the clues she needed to figure out what was going on.

No, no, no! Crap, no! She did *not* want to deal with this again. What the hell were Droogs doing in this part of town?

She rose up for a closer look. They weren't Droogs. At least, not the ones she usually battled. These were Columbia students, judging by their Gap outfits and leather laptop cases. But they were clearly hopped up on the same stuff that fueled the IV heads she knew and loved.

I should just run away. I should just sneak down the other way and race all the way to the bakery without looking back.

But even as she thought it, she knew she wouldn't do it. By now the more hyper of the Columbia Droogs had bounced to the left, revealing the pair's intended victim. It was a homeless man, small and disheveled, his age unknowable. The skin of his hands and face was so weathered and rough, it was hard to tell where the weave of his brown coat ended and his skin began. Gaia thought of the delicate detail on the body of the bird. . . .

She stood up straight and took a few shaky steps toward the trio.

"Aren't you scared? Aren't you scared out of your freaking mind?" the calmer of the two was demanding of the vagrant.

The man just stood there, mumbling to himself, his eyes focused but unseeing.

The bouncier guy bent down and picked something off the ground—a piece of gleaming green glass. "Use this, John. This will make him scared."

The other one, John, grasped the glass and turned the point toward the vagrant's face. "How do you like this? Isn't it pretty?"

The man tensed but otherwise remained in his hunched stance, chanting under his breath.

"What's he saying, John?"

"I don't know." John grabbed the man's chin with one hand and kept waving the jagged piece of glass beneath his nose with the other. "Speak up! Speak up or I'll cut you!"

"Leave him alone!" Gaia's voice seemed to blend with the breeze and fly away.

It wasn't quite the warning she'd been hoping to communicate, but at least she'd announced her presence.

The guys turned and looked at her. Their smiles widened.

"Oh, goody! A girl!" exclaimed the more hyper one. "Get her, John! Let's make *her* scream!" They turned from the homeless man, who slowly slid down the wall.

"Look how scared she is," John commented as they walked toward her.

Gaia immediately jumped into a fighting stance, which only made them laugh. "Run!" she shouted at the vagrant, but he remained in his crouched position, mumbling and rocking slightly. "Run, dammit!"

"How come you don't run, girlie? Aren'tcha scared?" The big, oafish one danced in front of her, giggling and making erratic grabbing motions with his arms. "We're gonna get you!" he sang out. "We're going to cut you up!"

He walked toward her, putting his hands on either side of his face and wiggling his fingers. "Boo! Raaah! *Oof!*"

Gaia kicked him in the stomach. He doubled over and fell to his knees.

John burst out laughing. Then he too raced toward Gaia, his hand with the glass shard leading the way.

Gaia steadied herself, suppressing the overwhelming urge to run away. As soon as he was in range, she deflected his arm with a chop block, then followed with a roundhouse kick to the groin.

The guy crashed to the ground, gasping from both effort and laughter. His fist had inadvertently closed around the shard, burying it halfway into his palm. He held up his hand and studied it, blood running in stripes down his arm. Then he burst out in a fresh spate of giggles. "Gordy," he called, waving his bloody hand. "Hey, Gordy! Look!"

The other guy was on his feet again. Before Gaia could turn around, he'd grabbed her from behind. She planted her feet and head-butted him backward as hard as she could. The force sent the back of his skull crashing into the wall behind him.

He let go of her and staggered around stupidly, his eyes bleary and his mouth still halfway curled in a smile. Finally he crumpled forward in a lifeless heap.

Something hard collided with Gaia's shoulder. "Ow!"

She turned around in time to see something else go flying past her. It crashed into the wall with a dull, shattering sound. John had found a crumbled bit of masonry and was using his good hand to fling bricks at her.

He launched another right at her head. Gaia dodged it and hit the ground. She tried to roll out of the way, but there was nowhere to hide. All she could do was shield her head and twist this way and that while John continued to pelt her with bricks, laughing as if he were playing a two-dollar carnival game.

Her forearms bruised and throbbing, Gaia somersaulted forward until she was right next to the guy, his arm raised for another throw. She quickly grabbed his wrist and forced it back, feeling the snap of a bone. The brick slid out of his hand and fell to the ground.

"I see it! I see it in your eyes!" he panted gleefully. "You're scared!"

The truth of his words hit her like another brick, and Gaia hesitated. In that instant he lunged forward and tackled her to the ground.

"Yep. Scared little girl," he continued babbling as he lay on top of her. His hands near useless, he crawled forward on his elbows until he was face-to-face with her. "I can feel your fear," he rasped, practically foaming with morbid delight.

Gaia felt panic rising inside her. It threatened to overtake her. But somehow she managed to force it back down. With a grunt of exertion she slammed her fist against the man's chin. His head shook from the impact. Then he opened his mouth and laughed out loud, blood trickling from the corner of his lips.

She punched him again and again, each time gaining more trajectory as the force of her blows slid him sideways off her. His face became a distorted mess of blood and spit and swollen flesh. But still he laughed harder and harder.

It was intensely freaky, but also annoying as hell.

Finally, after one last strike to his temple, his eyes rolled back into his head. His body gave a massive jerk and then flopped forward, completely motionless.

Gaia wriggled out from under him and lay on her back, panting heavily. A noise cut through the sound of her breathing—a low murmur growing louder and louder. It was the vagrant, who was still crouched against the opposite wall.

"Yea-though-I-walk-through-the-valley-of-the-shadow-of-death-I-will-fear-no-evil," he chanted, the words gradually growing faster and louder. "Yea-though-I-walk-through-the-valley-of-the-shadow-of-death-I-will-fear-no-evil."

Gaia rolled to her knees and staggered upright. "Are you all right?" she asked breathlessly.

His eyes snapped onto hers and he slowly rose to his feet. "Fear no evil!" he shouted, pointing at her. "Fear no evil! *Fear no evil!*"

She staggered backward, shaking her head. "Stop," she said. "Please stop." Everything around her seemed to sway and shimmer. She was passing out. Only she didn't want to. It was the creeping darkness she'd felt under the bed the night before. It was closing in on her, suffocating her.

Images swirled in front of her. The etched face of the vagrant. The bloody forms of her attackers. The tiny mound where the dead bird lay. The alley walls stretched and converged, then bent forward as if pinning her down.

Suddenly Skyler's face appeared in the mix. Only it wasn't Skyler. It looked just like him, but his forehead was creased in rage. And his eyes. His eyes were flaying her, ripping into her flesh.

"Gaia!" said a voice. "Evil!" said another.

Then, as if a thick black sheath had been pulled over her, everything went dark and silent.

GAIA OPENED HER EYES AND TRIED

Pitiful Form

to focus. All she could see was the fuzzy outline of something above her, like the splayed figure of a giant, five-legged spider. She blinked and refocused. It was a ceiling fan—the one in Skyler's bedroom.

She tried to rise up but only succeeded in tensing the sore muscles in her back and neck. Her limbs felt encased in lead; her stomach seemed to be simmering something. And judging by the intense throbbing, she wasn't entirely sure her skull was completely intact.

Eventually she managed to flop her head to the

side. Skyler was slouched in a chair beside her bed. His eyes were fixed on an invisible point in front of him, barely blinking, and his mouth was pursed, creating a small pocket of flesh right above his chin.

Flashes of memory flickered in her mind. She remembered the bird, the fight, the etched face of the vagrant. Skyler had been there, too. She could picture him standing over her, a look of intense fury contorting his princely features. She'd never seen him so angry. It was almost as if he hated her.

Gaia opened her mouth to speak, but all that came out was a croaky, rattling sound.

Skyler immediately jumped out of his chair and bent over her. "Gaia?" he asked. "Are you all right?"

Gaia stared at him. He looked and sounded genuinely concerned. No trace at all of the scary Skyler. "You. . . you're not mad at me?" she asked. For some reason her lower lip was trembling, and her voice had a chirpy, birdlike quality.

"No! Of course not," he said, pushing stray blond strands off her face. "I've been worried sick. I mean, Jesus God, what happened? I came out of the shower and you were gone. Then I go looking for you and find you grimy and bloody in the middle of some alley. What the hell happened?"

"I went to get bagels. For you."

Skyler's cobalt blue eyes drooped with compassion. "Gaia, you didn't have to do that. You needed to rest."

"I wanted to surprise you. Then there was this bird. It was dead." Her voice quavered as she remembered the small, `pitiful form` in her hand. "I went to move it and that's when I saw those guys picking on that man. I had to stop them."

"But that's not your responsibility," he said, stroking her forehead lightly. "You could have called someone. You could have come to me."

"There wasn't time."

"Gaia, you can't keep doing this to yourself. Don't get me wrong—you're amazing—but even you can't take on the whole city. I mean. . . who's going to look after you? It was a good thing I came along when I did. God knows what could have happened to you in that alley."

Gaia thought back to the `crazed stare` of the vagrant and shuddered.

"Promise me," Skyler murmured, grabbing up her right hand and holding it in both of his. "Promise me you won't ever leave here again without telling me where you're going."

A `renegade tear` stole down the center of her cheek, but Gaia didn't have the strength to stop it. "I just. . . wanted to surprise you."

"I know," he said, wiping her cheek with the back of his fingers. "It's okay. It just freaked me out is all."

Gaia felt a wave of shame. *What the hell was I thinking?* she scolded herself. *Skyler goes out of his way to keep me safe and help me recover from that fight, and how do I repay him? I sneak out and get into another one.*

"I'm sorry," she said, sobbing. "I'm so, *so* sorry."

"*Shhh*. It's okay." He continued stroking her hair as he talked, his voice a series of soft notes, like a lullaby. She could feel herself relaxing, crumbling under his kindness. How could she have ever thought him scary? Her vision of him had probably been just that—a crazy vision.

"Just promise me," he whispered. "Promise you won't leave me like that ever again."

"I promise," she replied. "I won't ever sneak out again. I swear."

Skyler smiled. "Good girl," he said, leaning down and kissing the top of her head. "That's all I wanted to hear."

Gaia felt overwhelmingly awkward, **mixture** hyperaware of **of** the fact that her breasts **fun** were completely visible through **and** the faded **fear** meshy material of her bra.

TENNIS BALL GOES UP. TENNIS BALL
goes down. Tennis ball goes up.
Tennis ball goes down. Tennis
ball goes up. Tennis ball bounces
off my head.

Autopilot Urge

"Ow!" Ed exclaimed, rubbing his skull while the Day-Glo green ball disappeared beneath his bed.

He heaved a long, loud sigh and glanced around his room. Now what?

God, he was bored. Not just bleary-eyed, yawn-in-your hand bored, but `bored to a near-pathological level`. This prison cell of a bedroom was about as mentally stimulating as a bowl of oatmeal. How could he have lived here all his life and not realized that?

He now knew, for instance, that there were 120 dingy white ceiling tiles in his room. There were also seventy-two slats in the miniblinds, six hairline cracks in the walls, and two cobwebs. Reading and listening to music just wasn't cutting it anymore. And watching TV or surfing the web only reminded him of the world outside that he was presently held back from. He was the virtual boy in the plastic bubble. Only without the thick saran wrap barrier and cheesy background music.

Ed wanted so badly to breathe outdoor air. He'd gladly trade the choking aroma of well-used bedsheets and that red zinger tea his mom kept bringing him for lung-fuls of car exhaust and the briny scent of urine-soaked sidewalks. But nooooo. Mom wasn't going to let him dangle his toe out of doors until the hospital called with the final test results.

He'd tried using reason. Why would the doctors release him if he wasn't completely better? Couldn't she tell by looking at him that he was fine? All he wanted to do was hang out at the coffee shop, not go deep-sea diving.

But his mom, of course, had all the answers. Ed knew precisely from whom he inherited his mouthi-ness. The doctors had released him into *her* care, she'd explain, patting him on the head like a puppy. Yes, he looked great, but there were still some scan results that hadn't been ready and they wanted to make sure there were no *internal* complications. Yes, she knew he missed his friends, but if they were truly his *friends*, they would understand. Besides, he was welcome to invite anyone he wanted to come visit.

Not a chance. He loved his mother. Really. And he appreciated her concern. Truly. But nothing would make him lose points faster than being babied by his mommy in front of his friends. And stuffing more people into this cramped, dull room wouldn't solve anything any-way. What Ed really wanted was to get out. To move.

He had fantasies of flying down a road on his skate-board. He imagined racing around the Central Park reservoir, slowing down only to check out any passing babeage. He even envisioned himself frolicking through a grassy field, kicking out his legs and lifting his arms to the sky, like some character in a feminine hygiene commercial. Whatever—he didn't care. He just wanted out of bed. Being cooped up like this was too much like being paralyzed again.

Of course he knew he could venture into the living room. But doing that would only encourage his mom to turn her fussing instinct up to eleven. And even though she seemed to mean well, Ed couldn't help wondering if she was enjoying this beyond the degree of concerned mother.

It irked him to hear her relate the whole drama to her friends when they dropped by with casseroles. She would lower her voice and relate the general details of his attack to choruses of gasps and sympathetic coos. Then she'd thank them profusely for their food offerings, her tone taking on a sticky sweet quality, as if she'd just gargled with maple syrup.

He wasn't sure why his mom's attitude bothered him. Maybe it was because when he'd had the skateboarding accident and was facing the possibility of permanent paralysis in his legs, she'd been nowhere near this understanding and attentive. Instead she'd become distant, and Ed had even sensed a veiled anger within her. He told himself she was probably mad at the world for allowing this to happen to her son. But deep inside he worried constantly that she was angry with *him*.

So naturally he was suspicious of this all-new, very-Brady mother.

The phone on his desk rang. Ed's heart practically skipped with glee. Along with gross motor skills, he was starving for any kind of social interaction.

"Hello," he sang merrily into the receiver.

"Uh, yes. Is this the Fargo residence?" came a somber, official-sounding voice. "This is Dr. Wagner at St. Vincent's Hospital. I'm calling with Ed Fargo's test results."

Ed sat bolt upright. "Yeah. Okay," he said breathlessly. "Just a second. . . *Mom!*"

Mrs. Fargo appeared in Ed's bedroom doorway, looking confused. "What? What's wrong?"

He held out the phone. "It's the hospital. They have my last test results."

She stepped forward and put the receiver to her ear. "Yes, this is Denise Fargo. . . yes. . . mm-hmm. . . yes. . . I see. . . ."

Ed bounced nervously on his bed. His mother's ultraserious tone and furrowed brow had him worried. Could the scans have turned up signs of infection? Would he be doomed to spend the next several days in his bedroom or—even worse—back at the hospital?

"Yes, Doctor. Thank you. . . Goodbye."

Ed watched as his mother slowly, carefully replaced the phone on its cradle. The suspense building inside him was reaching critical mass. If she left him waiting much longer, he could burst open, spewing tissue, red zinger tea, and Campbell's chicken and stars all over his bedspread. And then—then she'd *never* let him leave the apartment.

"Well?" he prompted.

"You're fine," she said finally. "The scans came back clear."

"*Waaahooo!* Fantastic! I can go back to school and everything, right?"

His mother smiled somewhat sadly. "I suppose so. But don't overdo it. No extreme sports for a while, okay?" She reached out and awkwardly patted him on the shoulder.

Ed jumped out of bed, threw his arms around his mother, and whirled her in a circle. She let out a little "oh" of surprise and then started laughing—a genuine, joyful laugh.

Ed was way too relieved to be mad anymore. Suddenly he felt real forgiveness toward his mother. So what if her doting seemed a little fake and self-serving at times—she tried, didn't she? Besides, he'd just been given a do-over. It was time to stop obsessing about the past.

"Now stop," his mom chided gently, looking slightly flushed as he set her back down on the floor.

"I told you to take things easy." She walked to the door, wobbling slightly. "I'll call you when I'm finished making lunch. In the meantime, try not to injure yourself while celebrating your recovery." She flashed him a wide, knowing smile and disappeared down the hallway.

"Yes!" Ed's fist rose into the air. He was sprung. Fancy-free. Back in action.

He should call someone. There was so much to do, so much to plan. Bouncing back onto his bed, he reached over and grabbed the phone off its cradle.

"It's a beautiful day. *Yeeeaaah*," he sang in his best Bono impression as his fingers punched out a number to the beat. "Don't let it get away. It's a beaut—" Ed paused suddenly, staring at his hand as if he didn't recognize it. He had just started dialing Gaia's number.

Oops.

Sighing defeatedly, he disconnected the line and replaced the receiver, his elation draining out of him like blood from a wound.

When is this going to stop? he wondered. Whenever big things happened to him, he instinctively wanted to share them with Gaia. How could he deprogram this annoying default setting? Why couldn't he automatically think of Mom or Kai or. . . Arnold Schwarzenegger?

Because Gaia and Big Things went together. Because nothing but Big Things happened when he and Gaia were girlfriend and boyfriend. She was, in fact, the very essence of Big Things.

Maybe he should just deal. It was natural he'd have these lapses, but his life was changing now. No more Gaia-the-girlfriend. No more Big Things.

Then again. . . had he been unfair to blame her for all the awful drama he'd been through while they were a couple? He'd had things happen before he met her—major things, like his skating accident. And obviously things were still happening now that she was just "a friend." Maybe that was just life, whether Gaia was a friend or something more.

So why not just call her? he wondered, staring at the cordless receiver lying in his hands.

No. Breaking up with Gaia hadn't solved his problems, but he still needed to limit contact with her. Pulling her in close again would only make things more complicated. She and Jake were on their way to happily-ever-after, no doubt filled with romantic strolls through the crime-infested areas of town, maybe a triathlon race down the aisle instead of the usual walk down it, and eventually lots of bodybuilding little kids. And Ed? Well, he had to take Kai to prom.

He was moving on to other things. Not as big but simpler and—hopefully—happier. Eventually he'd kick this autopilot urge to call Gaia first. Even if it took the rest of his life.

Friendship Squared

NO. NO! NOOOOOOOOOOO! GAIA SAT up, panting. She glanced around Skyler's bedroom and heaved a sigh of relief.

It had only been a dream. A bad one. Gaia couldn't quite puzzle the whole thing together, but it had something to do with being chased—or running after something she couldn't catch. The only detail she could remember was a pair of crazed, evil eyes. They weren't exactly following her, but everywhere she looked, they seemed to be peering out at her from the shadows.

She rubbed her eyes and massaged her temples, her hairline a swamp of sweat and alley grime. Eventually her pulse ceased its mad dash and her breath became deeper, more even.

Yay for me! she thought grimly. *Yet another surprise bonus from my newfound fear: nightmares!*

She'd had bad dreams when she was fearless, but never like this. There'd been no palpitations, no teeth gnashing, no gasping for breath. Mainly they were just these annoying little visions that needled her conscience, reminding her what a bad person she was.

Funny. She'd always wondered why they were called night*mares*. But in a way, it was like having wild horses stampede through her subconscious, kicking up all sorts of buried anxieties.

So this is what normal people deal with all the time, she thought. *What a scam.* It seemed especially unfair that after battling emotional (or, in her case, flesh-and-blood) demons all through their waking hours, they couldn't even get away from it all with a good night's sleep.

She slid out of Skyler's bed and stretched out her arms. She was still tired, but she was even more tired of resting. It was sweet of Skyler to insist she lie down after the alley skirmish, but her limbs were starting to feel droopy and waterlogged from being in bed so much. Besides, she didn't want to be alone with the image of those cold, cruel eyes still fresh in her mind.

She padded across the carpet and peeked into the living area. The door creaked a bit, making Skyler look up from his *Sports Illustrated.*

"Hey," he said, smiling. Gaia loved the way his face brightened as he saw her. "Feel better?"

She nodded. She still had that heady, slightly pressurized feeling, but overall her body and mind were being much more obedient. "Yeah, thanks. I guess it's probably safe to go home now."

Skyler frowned. "What?" He set down his magazine and pivoted around to face her. "Uh-uh. No way am I taking you back after everything that's happened."

"But you have stuff to do. Homework and—"

"So?" He made sweeping motions with his arms as if pushing aside invisible stacks. "I'm blowing it all off. The only thing that matters is getting you rested."

A snug warmth settled over Gaia. It was amazing how considerate Skyler was being toward her. But she couldn't take advantage of him any longer. "Thanks, but I really should check on some things. Besides, Jake's probably been trying to call me."

"I've got an idea." Skyler reached beneath the boxy end table and picked up Gaia's cell phone. "Here," he said handing it to her. "Why don't you check your messages and call people from here? Save yourself the minutes."

She gazed at him thoughtfully. Was he always this accommodating? Or was she somehow special?

Gaia turned on the phone and punched in her personal mailbox code. There came a series of clicks, followed by the faint drone of a recording coming on. "Message box empty," exclaimed a female operator a little too cheerfully.

What? She glared at the phone in her hand. *No one called? Not even Jake?* That couldn't be right. She vaguely remembered it ringing last night as they watched the movie.

She reentered the message box code and again the recorded voice unapologetically announced that it was empty. Whoever called last night must have hung up when she didn't answer. Either that or it had been a wrong number.

"What did they say?" Skyler asked, peering at her closely.

"Nothing," she replied, her stomach churning with self-pity. "No one called."

No one called. The thought echoed through her head like a siren. Jake hadn't even phoned once. Why? Wasn't he even the slightest bit worried about her?

Course not, she told herself. *All he cares about is playing Super–Secret Agent Man.* He was probably out with Uncle Ollie right now, learning all his tricks. First he'd master that unnerving coin thing. Then he'd take on a new moniker, like Loki Jr. or King Scumbag. Then he'd adopt the philosophy that relationships and personal loyalties meant nothing—that everything was secondary to supreme, dominating power.

Of course, maybe he'd already learned that. Maybe not calling was step one in Five Steps to a New Maniacal You.

She powered down the phone and squeezed it tightly in her palm. What did she expect? A voice mailbox full of pleas for forgiveness and invitations for dinner? Who exactly would be calling her right now? Her dad was too busy. Liz and Chris had quite the full, perfect life without her. Megan and the other FOHs had never really been that interested in including her. She'd effectively kicked Sam out of her life. And Ed, while not exactly out of her life, wasn't exactly *in* it either. So really, who would bother to call?

"Gaia?"

She suddenly realized that Skyler was talking to her. "What?"

"I asked if you were all right."

"I'm fine," she said, hoisting the corners of her mouth into a smile. She closed the phone with a snap and chucked it onto the nearby armchair.

"Fine?" he repeated doubtfully.

"Yeah. In fact, I'm fantastic," she added, bouncing onto the couch cushions. "Let's blow off everything, like you said. Let's just hole up here and have fun."

She was fooling no one. Not Skyler, not even herself. But she simply refused to acknowledge how pitiful her life was. There was one thing holding her upright at the moment: a flimsy, crooked buttress of pride.

That and Skyler.

She looked over at him and smiled. He was watching her with that spellbinding gaze of his. Equal parts concern and wonder and. . . something else. She couldn't quite grasp it.

"Okay, let's do it," he said reaching over and mussing up her already-tangled hair. "I'll go out to the kitchen and get us some fattening snacks. You find something for us to do out here—a game or a DVD or something."

She smiled at him appreciatively. "Sounds like fun."

Gaia continued smiling at Skyler as he hopped off the couch and disappeared around the corner to the kitchen nook. She'd never before met someone so willing to help her. It wasn't just friendship—it was like friendship plus. Friendship squared. Skyler always seemed to know what she needed and made it his all-absorbing mission to make it happen for her, completely subtracting his own needs from the equation.

How did she get lucky enough to find him just when she needed him most?

Power is so clearly an illusion.

When I was growing up, playing make-believe with all my pals, most of them fought over who would get to be Tarzan or Superman or Caine the Kung Fu Fighter—whatever lame fantasy we happened to be into at the time.

But not me.

I suppose that was one reason they liked hanging out with me. I never presented any real or imaginary threat. Like Darrell Howe would actually cry if he didn't get to be Batman, but I'd always let him. I didn't care. I would much rather be Commissioner Gordon.

To me, that was where the power was. Why would I want to run around bashing my head in when instead I could sit in an air-conditioned "office" (the tree house Dad had built for us, which was, in fact, air-conditioned) and have a superhero at my beck and call?

That's what people don't get.

It's always, ALWAYS better to be the person the hero answers to than the hero himself. After all, Caine had to answer to Master Kan. And considering that Tarzan and Superman would do anything their women told them to, didn't that mean Jane and Lois Lane were actually the more powerful ones?

It only makes sense that someone with supreme power would get others to do their dirty work. And let's face it, Tarzan, Batman, and Superman are all about dirty work. So why be one of the spies when you could be the martini-swilling boss who sends them their self-destructing mission instructions?

Right now I feel like I did then. As if I'm living out my childhood fantasies. I finally have the opportunity to get a true warrior under my control—an opportunity I'd be an idiot to pass up.

It was stupid for me to shower and let Gaia out of my sight, but it doesn't matter. She learned

her lesson. Besides, it allowed
me to drop off the hair sample
alone without raising her suspicions. And it gave me more time
to finish disabling her phone. No
more interruptions. The better to
work on you, my dear.

Actually, this is much more
fun than our stupid childlike
fantasies. This is real.
Remolding Gaia is like the most
thrilling rush ever. For the
first time, I know what real
power tastes like.

And you know what? It doesn't
make me feel like Commissioner
Gordon. It makes me feel like
King of the Universe.

THE SMALL BLUE DIE ROLLED ACROSS

the coffee table, stopping just before the edge. *Five.* Gaia bounced her small metal shoe around the **Freakazoid** game board and landed on Marvin Gardens, where, unfortunately, Skyler owned a big red plastic hotel.

"Damn," she muttered as she scooped up $1,200 (a good half of her stash) and handed the money to Skyler. Monopoly, she was quickly discovering, was not her thing. Her railroads and utilities had prevented her from going completely broke, but overall it was becoming clear that she did not make a good capitalist.

"So. . . tell me about your love life. Is Jake your first boyfriend?" Skyler asked as he casually tossed the bills onto his stack of play money. She thought it was funny how he never sorted or counted his cash. Maybe rich kids tended to take it for granted, even in games.

"No. There was a guy before him. Ed. He's just a friend now. And one other guy before that. Sam. That one didn't work out either," she said, reaching for the potato chips. "We had good chemistry, you know. But we disagreed on a lot of things. I was just too. . . different."

"Sounds complicated."

You don't know the half of it, Gaia thought wryly. She sat back on her heels and rubbed her eyes. Skyler wasn't kidding when he'd said he wanted to know everything about her. For the past couple of hours he'd been determined to hear her complete autobiography—from Huggies to high school. In a way, it was flattering that someone found her so interesting. She'd already told him about her father being in the CIA, but she'd decided not to risk much more truth than that. Still, it was tough editing out certain facts, avoiding certain topics altogether, and inserting the occasional bald-faced lie. He now knew, for instance, that her mom had been killed but that she'd been a victim of a hunting accident. And as far as he knew, she was an only child.

All that mental contorting was wearing her down. And she did feel guilty lying to him. But there was no need for Skyler to find out how freakazoid her real life was. Not yet.

"Hey, there." Skyler was watching her warily. "You should tell me to shut up if I get too nosy. I don't want to upset you."

"It's okay," Gaia reassured him. She loved it when he got all protective of her feelings. Was this what it was like to have a big brother? "Your turn."

Skyler rolled the dice and plunked his top hat onto the Chance square. "Go directly to jail," he read aloud. "Do not pass go. Do not et cetera, et cetera."

"Yes!" Gaia rejoiced. "Now get your butt in the slammer."

"Aren't you forgetting something?" He held up a crisp yellow card that showed a cartoon guy with wings flying out of a birdcage. "Get out of jail free," he read aloud.

"Crap!" she exclaimed, shaking her head. "See, this is why I prefer chess."

Skyler shrugged. "Same game, different board."

"That's not true at all. Monopoly's half luck. In chess you have to think ahead and—"

"Please!" he interrupted, rolling his eyes. "You sound just like Chris. Don't make me go all big brother on you."

"Oh, really? What will you do? What do you do to Chris?"

"Chris is easy. All I have to do is get his CD collection out of order and he throws a hissy. But you? You're more complicated. With you I'd probably have to resort to my Liz tactics."

"And they are. . . ?"

He leaned toward her, raising his hands in a menacing monster sort of way. "Tickling."

Gaia made a noise somewhere between a shriek and a laugh and leapt to her feet. Skyler followed, pursuing her around the apartment until she ended up trapped between the armchair and stereo cabinet.

She backed up against the wall, holding her elbows close to her rib cage. Never before had she felt such a mixture of fun and fear. As he slowly descended on her, his wriggling fingers inching toward her torso, she stood there cringing but laughing at the same time.

"I haven't even touched you yet," he exclaimed as she jerked sideways with a screeching giggle.

And suddenly, for the first time in her life, Gaia began to understand the absurd mystery of tickling. It wasn't so much the actual sensation of fingers digging into one's ribs but the anticipation of it that people responded to. She was laughing in expectation. A nervous, manic laugh, full of both dread and exhilaration.

"Don't worry," he murmured. "I'll go easy on you."

The next thing she knew, his hands were on her, fingertips burrowing beneath her arms. Gaia let out a loud burst of laughter cut short by a cry of pain.

Skyler instantly drew back his hands. "I'm sorry! Did I hurt you?"

"No. It's okay. I'm just sore is all." Gaia rubbed the tender spot on her side. Skyler's eyes were so full of pity and concern, the sight of them overwhelmed her. She had to turn away, focusing instead on the nubby weave of the carpet.

A somber air filled the room, as if someone had dumped a bucket of reality on their fun.

"I'm so sorry," Skyler repeated. He reached forward and lightly grasped her sweatshirt. "Here. Let me see."

Gaia moved her arms out of the way as he slowly lifted her shirt to reveal the wound.

"Jesus," he whispered, his fingertips gliding over the raised, credit-card-size welt. His knitted gaze met hers. "Are there more?"

She nodded.

"Show me."

Skyler led Gaia away from the wall and circled her, inching up her shirt to examine her back and sides. She stood there quietly, wincing as his warm hands touched her raw skin.

"Damn," he said under his breath.

She couldn't help feeling like some battered, neglected mannequin, but she wasn't going to object. Skyler had the firm-yet-soothing voice of a doctor administering an exam. Plus she liked gaining his sympathy. She wanted more of his big-brotherly concern.

"Come over here," he said, pulling her over to the bar stools. "We have to do something about this."

"No, I'll be okay. Really," she replied with a shrug. But even to her own ears her objection sounded weak.

"Stop it," he admonished. "I know those have got to hurt. Just let me take care of you." Setting her down on a stool, he began rummaging through a high kitchen cabinet, eventually pulling out a small tin box. He placed it on the counter and flipped back the lid, revealing a well-stocked first aid kit.

"Here, take off your shirt," he directed as he unscrewed the cap of a long metal ointment tube.

For a fraction of a second Gaia hesitated. Then she dutifully tugged the sleeves of her sweatshirt off her arms. Again Skyler had that undeniable air of authority—like a doctor or a judge. She was just the patient. The injured child. She would do as she was told.

Once her arms were freed, Skyler grasped the hem of her sweatshirt and helped her pull it over her head. The cool kitchen air breezed against her bare skin. Gaia felt overwhelmingly awkward, hyperaware of the fact that her breasts were completely visible through the faded meshy material of her bra. She might as well not have been wearing one at all. Under the pretense of being cold, she instinctively crossed her arms over her chest.

This was new. She'd never really been shy of nudity before. It wasn't that she loved her body—in fact, she'd always thought her long limbs and muscular build didn't suit a girl her age, making her seem more like a hard plastic action figure than a real live human. But before now—before fear—she'd just never seen what the big deal was all about.

And just as Gaia only understood nightmares and tickling since the onset of fear, only now did she understand why nudity was an issue. Sitting half naked under the yellow fluorescent lights, she couldn't shake the feeling of being on display. Was he judging her body? Did he think her breasts were too small? Too big? Did he think her bodybuilder arms were gross?

Get over it, she scolded herself. *He's only trying to help.*

Skyler didn't even seem to be watching her. He was

busy opening up bottles and little packets of cotton balls. Soon Gaia felt the `cold bite of alcohol` being swabbed against her scrapes. She flinched reflexively.

"Sorry," his voice murmured in her ear. "It'll sting a little."

After cleaning her cuts Skyler began rubbing a thick, warm cream into her wounds. His touch was deliberate yet gentle, and Gaia slowly relaxed into his care.

"Is that better?" he asked after a while, resting his hands on her shoulders.

"Yeah," she whispered. "Thanks."

"No problem." His fingers began gently kneading her muscles. "I bet you're sore all over, huh?"

"Mm-hmm," she agreed, leaning backward and surrendering into his soothing touch.

"I know just the thing." He gave her muscles one final prod with his thumbs and moved around to face her. "Come on," he said, gesturing toward the back rooms. "I'm giving you a bath."

"THIS WILL BE THE BEST THING for you." Skyler sat on the edge of his tub, shouting over the running water. "I always take one of these after a workout."

"Uh-huh?" Gaia said, fiddling as long as she could with her watch clasp. Finally she felt it was too obvious she was stalling. She slid it off her wrist and placed it on the counter.

Okay, she could easily convince herself that taking off her shirt was not a big deal. But completely undressing? *That* was a big deal. Yet for some reason, she didn't want to offend him by letting him see how uncomfortable she was. After all, he was only trying to take care of her. And he'd done nothing to make her distrust him.

As casually as she could manage, Gaia unbuttoned the front of her Levi's and pulled them down over her hips.

"You're going to love this," Skyler was saying, pouring a variety of oils into the tub. "You're being treated to the best Rodke-Simon bath products on the market."

"Really?" Gaia tried to sound casual as she yanked off her jeans, folded them neatly, and set them on the white tile counter.

"This one has lavender and juniper berries, which will help you heal," he said, holding up a small glass bottle before pouring in a thick teaspoonful. A glistening green oil slick formed on the surface of the water.

"Uh-huh. Good." She carefully pulled her sock off her left foot and folded it, too.

"And this one has sage, which is great for sore muscles."

"Right. Great." She couldn't put it off any longer.

Just do it, she told herself. *It's only Skyler, for chrissake. Quit being such a prude.*

Gaia reached back, unhooked her bra, and quickly pulled it off. *Okay. That wasn't so bad,* she told herself as she placed it on the rest of her clothes. She took a quick peek toward Skyler. He was busy adding a salty substance to the bathwater. Now for the big finish. She took a deep breath of air and courage and slid off her underwear. *There,* she thought, adding it to the teetering clothing pile. She'd done it. She was now completely naked. Totally exposed. Body parts on parade.

But so what? she asked herself. What was the big deal? Naked wasn't bad. It was natural. It was freeing. It was—

"You ready?"

Eep. Gaia jumped slightly. She turned and faced Skyler, who was now looking right at her. At her eyes. Thank God, he was looking into her eyes. But what was he thinking? She searched his gaze for any flickers of amusement or disgust but found nothing. But then, what did she know? Ever since she had gained fear, it had been that much tougher to read people. She found she couldn't quite separate what was clearly there from what she *feared* might be there.

Gaia fought off the urge to cover herself with her arms, then wondered what else to do with them. She had no pockets or belt loops or anywhere else to place her hands. How did one strike a natural pose while in the buff?

Skyler smiled and gestured toward the bathtub. "Go ahead. Get in before it gets cold."

"Okay. Thanks," she said quickly. As casually as she could, she walked past him and stepped over the side of the tub, settling into the steamy bath. Skyler hadn't been exaggerating about the strength of the bath products. It was like being dunked in a giant cup of tea.

She stretched out her legs and leaned her head back against the side of the tub. Soon she could feel her muscles become warm and loose. She couldn't remember the last time she'd taken a long, relaxing bath. The boardinghouse had only showers, and hot water was controlled like war rations. And even if she could have bathed, Gaia typically chose not to, preferring quick, no-nonsense showers. She never was very good to herself.

Ahhh. She closed her eyes and inhaled the pungent vapors.

"How does it feel?" Skyler asked from where he sat at the foot of the tub.

"Fantastic."

"Told you."

She was just wondering why Skyler was still there when she suddenly felt his hands on her shoulders. She jerked in surprise.

"*Shhh*. Relax," he murmured, his fingers kneading her sore muscles. His strong fingers raked down her back, smoothing out kinks and cramps.

Stop the freaking, she told herself. *Skyler probably doesn't even care that you're totally nude. He's just helping you feel better—like a doctor or masseur. Nudity comes with the job.*

His hands were now traveling down her arms, smoothing out her triceps, her biceps, everything in between. He was right. It was helping—majorly. She moaned in pleasure, giving in to the sensations. She didn't even mind when his left fingertips accidentally brushed the side of her breast.

It felt like Skyler was literally, physically *fixing* her, remolding her into a better version of herself. She could practically hear the old theme from *The Six Million Dollar Man* start up in the distance. *We can rebuild her. We can make her better than she was before. Better. . . stronger. . . less annoying. . . da, da, da DAH!*

"Does it hurt here?" Skyler murmured into her ear. He'd moved up to her neck, massaging the skin with firm, circular patterns.

"Mmm. Yeah. A little," she said, her head bobbing from the movement. "Probably from when that big guy grabbed me from behind."

There was a long pause and then Skyler spoke again, his tone slightly halting as if he were carefully inspecting each word before using it. "Um, Gaia?

Don't take this the wrong way, but. . . do you purposefully get drawn into fights?"

"No," she replied, swishing her hands back and forth in the water to create waves. "They just seem to find me."

"But why give in? Why not take off for safety? Wouldn't that be the smart thing to do?"

Gaia stared down at the bruises on her knuckles. *Sometimes I do run, Skyler.* She remembered taking off from the park that time, leaving Jake to deal with all those IV heads himself. And the other time she'd run away—when Ed ended up getting stabbed. That had been the opposite of smart. That had been the most selfish, stupid thing she'd ever done.

"I just try to help," she said, rather lamely. "That's all."

"Do you"—again he paused cautiously—"do you think it's fun?"

"No!"

"Never? You don't get the slightest bit of satisfaction out of it?"

"Well. . . yeah. I mean, sometimes they deserve it. Jake says—"

"*Jake?* Your boyfriend? He knows you do this?"

"Y-Yeah," she replied, sensing she'd made some mistake.

"And he's okay with this?"

"Yeah. Sometimes he even helps me out. He's also a black belt and—"

"Wait. Wait a minute," Skyler interrupted. "You mean you and he go out and take on bad guys like some sort of crime-fighting duo? Does he put you up to this?"

"No!" Gaia's body seemed to be tensing all over again. "He doesn't have to do it at all. He just likes helping me—"

"What? He *likes* it?" Skyler's strong, warm hands left her back. She felt suddenly cold and exposed.

"No. I mean, yes. I mean. . ." Gaia sighed. She had a sudden urge to sink below the waterline and disappear. "He's just looking out for me is all."

"Fine. Whatever." The disappointment in Skyler's voice was making her feel guilty. "Look, I don't mean to pry. I just think that. . . if he was really looking out for you, he'd try to stop you from getting into those situations."

Gaia hugged her knees to her chest, unsure of what to say. There was no way she could make Skyler understand without opening the giant Pandora's box that was her life story. No way to convince him that Jake wasn't some crazy thrill seeker.

She knew how it sounded to him, but he couldn't be more wrong about Jake. He wasn't this nutcase who fancied himself her loyal sidekick. He was her rock, her confidant, her understanding boyfriend. Maybe he was a bit too caught up in the intrigue of her life, but he still cared for her. He only wanted what was best for her.

Right?

"Take care!"

What nitwit starting using that phrase as a fond farewell? *Take care?* Take care of what? My teeth? My cuticles? A pet gerbil? Of course, a sane person would probably point out that these well-wishers simply want me to look out for myself in general. But even then, why? What the hell do they know that I don't? "There will be loads of anvils falling onto Twelfth Street tomorrow. . . . Take care!" I mean, how freaking demanding. Why are they ordering me to take care of my own self? If it's social politeness they're after, wouldn't it be nicer for *them* to offer to take care of *me*?

Right. Like that would happen. People would probably consider a wild sewer alligator more in need of concern. "Good ol' tough freak-of-nature Gaia. Don't bother look-ing after her. She can fight."

Yeah? So? I'm so sick of everyone—including my dad and Jake—assuming that just because I

can kick cinder blocks into rub-
ble, I must be a paragon of self-
sufficiency. That my black belt
in karate and my standoffish personality mean I don't need anyone, ever.

Um. . . hello? Let's riddle
this one together, shall we? The
fact that I can fight means I
tend to end up in fights, which
means (now bear with me here)
that I'm more likely to end up
hurt/in trouble/possibly needing
help. Got me? And my tendency, at
least in the past, to shoo away
the social butterflies? Well,
that's just textbook defense
strategy, isn't it? We loner mis-
fits who act all tough are really
just soggy marshmallows on the
inside. We may snarl, "Get lost!"
but what we're really saying is,
"Love me, hold me, be my best
friend."

Maybe I never really felt
these insecurities when I was
fearless, but they were there.
And now that I can sense them,
it's not this small shadow being

cast on my self-image. It's more
like. . . Freddy Krueger massaging my intestines. It hits me so
hard, it hurts.

The real fact is, I need someone. I always did. In a way, getting the fear gene was like
yanking off a heavy, blinding
helmet, allowing me to see how
insane the world really is and
how alone I really am. It's
scary. I mean, I'm only seventeen. Why should I be made to
look after myself? It isn't fair.

Lately, in my darkest moments,
when I can feel the evil and
despair crushing in from all
directions, I've fantasized about
being locked up somewhere—someplace where I'd be safe, where
others would have to look after
me at all times. I've even envied
those people stuck in institu-
tions. Yes, it's true. Me, Gaia,
supposed Queen of all Miss
Independents, actually dreamed of
a rubber-room existence. It just
seemed so nice and simple. People
bringing me meals, changing my

bed, always talking in those hushed kindergarten teacher voices. I wouldn't have to go anywhere or do anything but watch *7th Heaven* reruns and make lanyards.

But maybe I don't need to go quite that far. Maybe all I need is someone willing to look after me. Someone who sees that I'm not all that together—despite all the kicking and punching skills—and could use a little guidance.

And right now I'm thinking that someone could be Skyler.

He needed
to grab
the **absolute**
city by
mess
the scruff
of
of the
neck and
a
shake
Gaia out
girl
of it.

"YES, THAT'S RIGHT. RODKE.

Wonderful World of Rodke

R-o-d-k-e." Jake paced around the sidewalk, holding his cell phone to one ear and covering the other with his hand. "My name is Gerald Rodke and I'm trying to locate my cousin, Skyler Rodke, who's a student there. My dad, his uncle. . . uh. . . Fester, is in the hospital. It's really bad. His last wish is to see his nephew, but we don't have Skyler's current address or phone number. Couldn't you maybe—?"

"I'm sorry," the university operator replied through her nostrils, "but we cannot give out students' personal information."

"I know. I know. It's for security and all. You need to protect them from all the crazies out there. But see, I'm his *family*. This is a family emergency. A matter of life and death."

"I'm sorry." Jake hated the way she kept saying that without really meaning it.

"All right," he said, exhaling heavily. "I'm going to level with you. I'm not really his cousin." There was a silence on the other end of the line. Finally he'd gotten her to really listen. "My name is Agent Montone and I'm with the CIA. I need to speak with Skyler Rodke about a highly classified subject—"

Jake heard a series of clicks followed by the low mournful pitch of the dial tone.

Okay, so he really hadn't expected that to work, but *come on*! Why couldn't he get a break? He needed some sort of lead. A tip-off from one of Skyler's friends. A phone call from Gaia. A neon billboard that flashed "This way to Skyler's." Hell, he'd settle for someone telling him which freaking direction to walk in.

The day was already half over, but when he last called Gaia's' boardinghouse, Suko had said she still wasn't home. It occurred to him that she might be lying for Gaia, but that didn't seem her style.

He had the distinct feeling that time was running out. Something awful was happening to Gaia, but he didn't know what. Or where, when, how, or why.

But he did know who.

Jake chucked the phone into his bag and stood back on the sidewalk, glaring at the nearby buildings. Then, in a sudden burst of decisiveness, he turned and started running northward.

He was tired of fooling around. Tired of tiptoeing about waiting for a clue to land in his lap. He needed to grab the city by the scruff of the neck and shake Gaia out of it. Forget undercover methods and being all "professional." He needed to deal with the problem the only way he knew how: direct and in-your-face. This wasn't just an assignment. This was Gaia.

He hurried down the still-slick sidewalks, tapping into his bottled-up rage to use as fuel for his weary, sleep-deprived body. Meanwhile those maddening thoughts he'd been trying to keep at bay crept back into his consciousness, unspooling through his mind like a disjointed and extremely annoying infomercial.

Somebody had gotten to Gaia, and Oliver seemed to think there was a Rodke connection. What that connection was, Jake had no idea. But it pissed him off.

Gaia had been his. They had been through so much together, understood each other to an almost basic, molecular level. But lately Gaia hadn't been Gaia anymore. According to Oliver, her genetic code had been tampered with. And what infuriated him to no end was that it had happened on his watch. He should have sensed it coming, but he didn't. He let her down.

Jake's anger propelled him all the way to Fifth Avenue. Soon the Rodkes' elegant apartment building zoomed into view like an exterior shot from a movie. The Wonderful World of Rodke. It looked too stylish to house dark secrets. But then, he reminded himself, weren't all the pretty, colorful snakes always the most poisonous?

A doorman in a neat blue suit was standing under the front awning. He watched Jake warily as he approached. Jake found himself wishing he'd cleaned himself up a bit before coming.

"Hi," he greeted casually. "I'm here to see the Rodkes."

"You're from the Village School?" the man asked, taking in Jake's scruffy clothes and two-day whisker growth.

"Uh. . . yeah," Jake replied. "I go to school with Liz and Chris."

The man pulled open the front door. "Seventeenth floor," he said, motioning with his free hand toward the elevator.

That was easy, Jake thought as the elevator began to rise with a soothing hydraulic whir. *Could they be expecting me?*

The elevator glided to a stop and the doors parted, revealing the Rodkes' gray-and-beige-striped vestibule. Jake stepped out and knocked on the black-lacquered front door.

Liz opened it and beamed at him in surprise, her front teeth gleaming in the chandelier light like a row of square pearls. "Jake! What are you doing here?"

"Looking for Gaia."

Liz's face fell. "Still? Didn't you find her last night?"

"No," he replied, feeling a `prick of irritation.` "Listen. I know she's with Skyler and I've got to talk to her. It's really important. Could you tell me where he lives?"

Liz crossed her arms over her chest and leaned against the door frame. "How do you know she's with Skyler?"

"I. . . I just know."

"Uh-huh," she muttered, wavy lines appearing on her forehead. "What's going on, Jake?"

"Nothing. I mean. . . okay. Yes, something is going on, but I can't tell you what." Jake tried to contain his irritation inside his clenched fists. Why did she insist on giving him the third degree? Wasn't it obvious that this was important? "I really need to find Gaia. Please, just tell me where Skyler lives."

"I can't do that." She shook her head. "Sorry."

There was that word again. Jake held back the urge to begin shouting. "Why?" he asked, taking a deep breath. "Why can't you?"

"Look, my family is just really protective about stuff like that. It's for security reasons."

"But this is really important!" He didn't even try to disguise his exasperation anymore. It bothered him to hear her talk about the importance of Skyler's security when Gaia could be in major trouble.

"How am I supposed to know that?" Liz countered, her own voice rising. "You won't even tell me what this is all about!"

Jake reached up and lightly pounded his fist against the doorjamb. "I told you," he said in a low, measured voice. "I need to talk to Gaia. I'm really worried about her and she's been out all night. With your brother."

Liz raised her right eyebrow. "Oh, really? So she

spent the night with Skyler and now you want to go over there and *talk*? Yeah, right. I see where this is headed. You think I'm going to let you go over there and pick a fight? Forget it!"

"No! It's not that way at all!" Jake exclaimed.

But Liz just kept shaking her head, her wry expression cemented to her features. God, he was an idiot! What was he going to do now?

Of course he wanted to beat up Skyler. He wanted to pound him into a puddle of grease. He wanted to rearrange his pretty-boy face until he looked like someone in a Picasso painting. But he wouldn't— at least, not as long as Gaia was okay. But how was he supposed to convince Liz he was more concerned with Gaia's safety than her fidelity? He couldn't. Not without saying even worse things about her brother.

But he wouldn't give up now. Liz was his last and only chance. Somehow he had to make her understand.

Artfully Subtle

PARADISE. EDEN. VALHALLA. FIFTH Avenue. It was all the same.

Megan cast an approving eye over the fastidiously manicured lawns, the opulent stone buildings, and the postcard views of Central

Park. Even the pigeons looked better over here. Their feathers seemed brighter and well pressed—as if each bird had been carefully outfitted by Chanel.

Yep, this was definitely her place. Other people might feel a calling to go to Africa, to help out the animals or whatever. But she'd always known she'd end up here, in this zip code. After all, these were her people. They knew all about the better things in life. Which, let's face it, made them better than just ordinary people.

Like Mr. Rodke. He'd heard that the prom committee was trying to raise money for decorations and had promised a sizable donation. Now they could finally get the good stuff instead of the cheap paper and plastic things. Obviously he didn't want his son and daughter to have to suffer a cheesy prom. And thanks to his generosity, everyone in the Village School would benefit. Now if they could just get Amy van Cline to shut up about having a medieval May fest theme. *Please!*

Megan knew she'd made a really good impression on Mr. Rodke over the phone. As president of the prom committee, she'd thanked him for his thoughtful contribution and even made a comment about it not being that long since his own prom. He'd laughed appreciatively.

At first he offered to have Liz bring the check to school, but Megan managed to change his mind, insisting that Liz had enough to do and that she didn't mind picking up the check herself on Saturday since she was going to be in neighborhood.

Now she was finally going to get her foot in the Rodke door—so to speak. Although it was rather embarrassing that she'd had to resort to such tactics for an invite.

Unlike Gaia Moore, she thought, lifting her chin in indignation. How that absolute mess of a girl had managed to worm her way into their favor was beyond her. Maybe this was Chris and Liz's way of rebelling against their upbringing? Whatever. She'd just have to work on the dad. She'd finagle a dinner invitation and prove that she was worthy of their friendship. Mr. Rodke obviously wanted the best for his kids. He'd make sure she got into their social scene. Chris and Liz would have no choice.

Really, it would be for the best. Down the line they would have eventually grown weary of Gaia's crudeness, anyway. This way she could be there when they cut Gaia off, and together the three of them could laugh at how messed up she was.

Megan stopped a few yards from the Rodke building and checked her reflection in her pink Estée Lauder compact. She smoothed the flips in her hair and practiced her high-society smile—warm in a closed, unimpressed sort of way. She had to keep her eagerness in check and prove she was one of them.

"Good afternoon," she said brightly as she approached

the doorman. "I'm a representative of the Village School, here to see the Rodkes."

He frowned slightly. "Yes," he said after a slight pause. Then he opened the door and gestured inside. "Seventeenth floor."

Okay, that *was rude,* she thought, stepping into the gleaming wooden lift. Someone should teach him a thing or two about proper deference.

As the elevator approached the seventeenth floor, a commotion of muffled, yelling voices cut through the steel walls. The doors opened and the volume intensified. Megan stepped out into the vestibule and froze, her `artfully subtle` smile transmuting into a gaping stare.

Directly in front of her stood Liz Rodke and Jake Montone in some sort of angry face-off. Liz's hands rested on her hips, which were cocked up to the right, the same angle as her head. Meanwhile Jake stood in a clenched, pleading stance. Arms bent in front of him, fists pressing against each other.

"How do you know Gaia slept over at my brother's apartment? She could be anywhere!" Liz shouted.

"I just know," Jake replied in a low sizzle.

*Hell*o. Megan's smile returned, wider than before. *What's this about Gaia sleeping over at Skyler's?*

This was turning out even better than she'd imagined.

"Well, there's no way I'm going to let you go over there and start trouble! Why don't you just—" Liz paused, finally noticing Megan over Jake's shoulder. "Hi!" she greeted, a little too loudly and overly enthusiastic. "You've come for the check, right?"

Megan nodded, still too stunned for speech.

"Excuse me, Jake," Liz said in mock sympathy. "I've got some important family business to attend to. Just a moment, Megan. I'll go get the check."

As she stalked away, Jake slowly crumpled forward as if in defeat. Then, exhaling heavily, he walked over to the elevator and gave the down button a harsh jab.

Megan stepped up beside him, a morbid curiosity straining at the inside of her chest. "I'm sorry," she said, putting a hand on his forearm. "I couldn't help overhearing all that."

He tensed at her touch, his cheek muscles doing a rhythmic spasm.

"I hate to say I told you so," she went on, "but we've been trying to warn you about Gaia for a while now."

Again he said nothing, his eyes glaring at the elevator doors as if trying to burn through the metal.

"She doesn't deserve someone like you. She's too—"

There was a loud, inappropriately cheerful *ding* as the elevator returned to the floor. Then the doors parted and Jake marched inside, wrenching his arm out of her grasp in the process.

"Bye, Jake," she called merrily. "See you at school!" Her view of his slouched form narrowed with the closing doors, then disappeared entirely.

Gaia and Skyler? she thought, twirling back toward the Rodkes' posh entranceway. She bounced in her Blahniks, feeling absolutely giddy.

She really wished Liz would hurry up with that stupid check. Suddenly she had a lot of important calls to make.

GAIA SHIFTED HER POSITION ON

Skyler's couch, rearranging the plush robe to cover her bent legs. Then she closed her eyes, letting the raspy vigor of the violins in Tartini's *The Devil's Sonata* ebb and flow through her body.

Scum Magnet

It had been the only thing in his CD collection that appealed to her. Everything else was too sad, too angry, too. . . J.Lo. Skyler's music seemed to be all twenty-something angst. Whiny singing over whiny guitars. Hard rock bands with their bullet-train bass lines and Cookie Monster vocals. Then, stuck in among the testosterone tracks, was a collection of Italian baroque music. Who knew?

"You sure you don't want one of these?" Gaia opened her eyes and saw Skyler emerge from the kitchen, rattling a glass of a sparkly, cinnamon-colored liquid. "I make a mean highball."

"No, thanks," she replied. "I don't drink."

"You sure? I mean, I think it's great you don't drink and all, but it might help you relax."

"It's okay. Really. I'm relaxed."

It was true. She felt immensely better after her bath. Completely unwound, yet mentally invigorated. Even the ill-defined dread in the pit of her stomach had subsided to a dull rumble, like the nagging feeling you get when you forgot something important.

"So where were we?" Skyler muttered, settling into the armchair. He draped his right leg over one armrest and perched his left elbow on the other, lazily holding up his drink. Again Gaia was struck by his boy-king manner, that captivating mixture of authority and rakishness. "Oh, yeah, you were telling me who you hang out with at school—besides your boyfriend."

Gaia shrugged. "I don't know. Mainly Liz and Chris."

Gaia Moore, this is your life! She still couldn't understand why Skyler found her so fascinating. But she had to admit she liked his interest. It made her feel significant somehow—more valuable.

"What about before we moved here?" Skyler went

on. "Surely you had lots of friends before we came."

"Not really. Just Jake and—" She paused. She'd been about to say Ed, but that wasn't exactly true. He was special to her—he'd always be special to her—but Ed hadn't been a real friend for a while now. Even before the Rodkes had come onto the scene, they'd been in a self-imposed separation. "Just Jake."

"No girlfriends?"

Gaia twisted the fingers of her left hand. She thought of Mary, lying in a pool of blood. Of Heather, her beautiful blue eyes dimmed and unseeing. Then she thought of the FOHs with their collection of smirks, sneers, and phony smiles, all expertly crafted just for her.

"I guess I don't get along with girls as much as I do guys," she answered finally. "I don't really know why."

"Probably because you're so strong. I don't just mean bodywise. I mean you have a strong presence, too." He paused and took a sip of his drink. "Plus you're beautiful. Those two things intimidate other girls."

She stared down at her split, ragged fingernails. A minuscule smile was tugging the ends of her mouth. She'd been called beautiful before but never believed it. Yet she liked the way Skyler rattled it off as if he were simply stating a fact.

Gaia had never really thought of her effect on other girls before. Maybe he was right. Maybe the fact that she didn't care about the FOHs' opinion of her—

or at least didn't *used* to care—was like an unspoken challenge to them. That would explain their inexplicable need to make her life even more of a `purgatory.` Leave it to Skyler to put it so succinctly. He had a talent for taking all the scraps she fed him about her life and turning them into a full, comprehensible portrait. She had a sudden urge to ask *him* all about herself, since he obviously understood things a lot better than she did.

Her thoughts were interrupted by a loud, harsh buzzer, `like the "time's up" signal on a game show.` She jumped into a sitting position, her heart jerking sideways in her chest.

Skyler stood and grasped her shoulder reassuringly. "It's okay. That's just the door. Probably the laundry service returning your clothes."

"Right," she said, smiling sheepishly.

Christ, when am I ever going to get a grip? she wondered. *Other people have fear and they don't startle at things like shoelaces and doorbells. Could they have made a mistake at Rodke and Simon? Did they splice too much fear into my matrix?*

The mere thought of such a thing filled her with more prickly panic.

Skyler set down his drink and peered through the peephole in the door. "Yeah. It's the service."

Gaia watched him open up, heard the muted mumbling of a conversation, and saw him press a few bills into someone's outstretched palm. Soon after, a small bundle of folded clothing was deposited into his arms.

"Here you go," he said, closing the door and handing her the pile. "Why don't you get dressed and we'll go eat something? There's a great pizzeria nearby. They make an amazing anchovy-and-tomato pie."

"Okay."

She went into the bedroom and pulled on her clothes, which were still `toasty warm` from the dryer. So nice of Skyler to take care of that. If it had been left up to her, she would have stayed in the same smelly, grimy outfit for the rest of the day. But Skyler knew what was best. He knew exactly how to take care of her.

Like now, for instance. She didn't really feel hungry, but it was probably a good idea for her to eat. He was looking out for her needs, something no one had really done since her mom died. She would go and eat her pizza like a good girl. She'd even ignore the fact that she hated anchovies.

As they trudged down the stairs, Skyler draped his arm around her shoulders. "I'm glad you stayed over," he said.

She met his smile and mirrored it. "Me too."

Again Gaia was struck by an intense gratitude toward him. For taking care of her. For trying to understand her. For making things easy when they'd been hard for so long. Without even thinking about it, she tilted her head sideways, resting it against his shoulder. Skyler tightened his grip on her, pulling her closer.

They descended the rest of the way in their Siamese-twin-like stance, separating when they reached the front door. As they stepped outside into the moldy, postrain air, Gaia was surprised to see the lavender light of approaching dusk. It was later than she'd thought.

They hastily crossed at the corner. The light was even dimmer on the other side of the street. Shadow upon shadow mottled the sidewalk like a giant camouflage pattern. Even the air was cooler. She put her hands in her pockets, pulling her unzipped jacket tighter around her chest.

All of a sudden something moved in the darkness nearby. A hulking shape emerged from the mouth of an alleyway, making straight for them.

Gaia sucked in her breath. What now? More IV heads? Muggers? Rapists? Could she not even go get pizza without being attacked?

"Skyler, watch out!" she called as she jumped into a fighting stance, her eyes fixed on the thug lumbering toward them.

"What the. . . ?" Skyler stopped, glancing up nervously. He obviously hadn't seen the guy coming. Of course not. He was used to walking down a street without being molested, while Gaia, scum magnet that she was, had learned to keep a lookout.

She maintained her defensive posture, although somewhat shakily. Her heart was beating so violently, it made her whole body throb. She watched as the man slowly came into view.

A tattered brown coat. Skin like paper that had been crumpled and resmoothed. Bloodshot eyes sunken with misery.

It was the homeless man from before. The one she'd saved from the hopped-up university kids.

Gaia's arms drooped limply at her sides as he shuffled toward her. He was obviously not a threat, but for some reason, she couldn't help feeling wary. What did he want? To thank her? To ask for more help? Beg for money?

The man stopped a foot away from her and stared directly into her eyes. Then he raised a crinkly hand and pointed right at her. "Be. . . thy brother's keeper." His gravelly voice contained a note of warning—or admonishment. She couldn't tell which.

"What?" she asked.

"Come on." Skyler gripped her arm and tried to tug her down the sidewalk with him. "Just keep walking."

But Gaia couldn't move. She stood fixed in place, spellbound by the intensity in the man's gaze.

"Be thy brother's keeper!" he said again, his pitch now clearly angry.

Brother's keeper. . . It echoed through her, awakening some subterranean fear.

Although she stayed frozen upright, Gaia felt like she was falling. Something inside her—some vital cog in her inner machinery—seemed to break, and the scene in front of her warped and decelerated, as if gradually sapped of power.

It was like watching a `nightmare at half speed`. She could see the haggard face of the vagrant, his expression full of harsh accusation. It loomed and stretched before her, frightening her. Then Skyler stepped into view, his features kindled with rage. The two faces swirled around each other, splintering and melding, until a new face emerged. One from her conscience. A beautiful innocent face.

Her brother. D.

Poor D., she thought, *out in the world—this horrible, treacherous world.* He was the only person besides Skyler who had always been good to her. And what was she doing to help him? Nothing. Not a thing.

She was not her brother's keeper. The man had every right to be yelling at her.

"Be thy bro—"

"No!" Gaia shouted, closing her eyes and covering her ears with her hands. "Stop it! Leave me alone!"

Now Skyler was yelling at the man. She could hear his muffled shouts over the man's scolding, like cracks of lightning amid dull thunder. Then everything went silent.

"Come on, Gaia. It's over," came Skyler's muted voice. "He's gone."

She opened her eyes. Her gaze darted about, but there was no sign of the vagrant anywhere. She relaxed slightly, letting Skyler pull her hands from her ears, holding them in his own.

"The best thing to do is ignore people like that. He was just a lunatic. He didn't know what he was saying."

Gaia nodded weakly. She couldn't tell him he was wrong. The man knew. He was warning her. Rebuking her. Something awful could be happening to D. this very minute. It was her premonition come true.

"Look at you. You're shaking," he observed, running his hands up and down her arms. "Let's go find a quiet booth at the pizza place and get you something to eat."

"No." Gaia shook her head. "I'm sorry. I really don't feel well. Couldn't we just. . . go back?"

Skyler brushed the hair off her face and stared at her worriedly. "All right," he said softly. "Sure."

He draped an arm about her shoulders and gently steered her back to his apartment building, somehow sensing her need for physical support.

But of course he did. Skyler always knew exactly what she needed.

"COME ON, TELL US. WHAT WERE THEY

Subversive Camaraderie

arguing about?"

Megan ignored her friends' round, pleading stares. She gave a small, evasive grin and sat back against the leopard-print upholstery, toying with the hot pink paper umbrella in her mai tai.

She enjoyed prolonging this moment. Let them snarl and beg and huff impatiently. She was in no hurry. After all, gossip like this should be savored, doled out in tiny morsels instead of carelessly dumped in a pile.

After a while she set down her drink and sat forward again. Her eyes roved around the circular bamboo booth, meeting the others' hungry gazes. "Liz wanted to know why Jake was so sure Gaia had slept over at Skyler's last night."

Megan felt a victorious thrill as the rest of the girls gasped in unison.

"Oh my God! Gaia and Skyler?"

"No way!"

"What did Jake say?"

"He said he just knew," she replied calmly.

More gasps and murmurs of astonishment.

"And," she continued, tossing her hair over her shoulder, "he was demanding to know Skyler's address. I think he was hoping for some big show-down, but Liz was too smart for him. She refused to give it over."

"Poor Jake," Laura crooned.

"Yeah. I can't believe Gaia!" Tina exclaimed, shaking her head.

Megan frowned at her. "*I* can. This is typical man-grubbing Gaia. The girl must have some weird complex that makes her go after every hot guy on the island. And this time she thought she was so all that, she tried to add another guy to her collection without breaking it off with her current boyfriend first."

"Poor Jake," Laura murmured again.

"Yeah, well, he's not standing for it. And I say good for him." Megan twirled the tiny umbrella between her thumb and forefinger. "The question is, what does this mean for us?"

Laura sucked in her breath. "Jake doesn't have anyone to take to prom!" she exclaimed happily.

Megan rolled her eyes. "*Duh!* I'm talking about the bigger picture here. Don't you see? This fits perfectly into Operation Revenge." She glanced around the crowd in the tiki bar and then leaned forward, lowering her voice. "What we need to do now is tell the whole school about Gaia's slutty ways."

The rest of the table exchanged sly looks, nodding and murmuring their approval. A sense of subversive camaraderie spread through the group. Megan could feel it gathering weight, crystallizing their sense of purpose.

This could very well be the best day of her life.

"Gaia won't know what hit her," she went on, smiling with pure glee. "Even if she dares to show up at prom now, she won't be very welcome. We'll make sure of that."

Gaia felt
the familiar
prick of
dread,
like a
hypodermic
to the
gut.

**fish
sticks
and
sanka**

GAIA BALANCED ON THE TILE COUNTER-

Bound and Gagged

top in Skyler's bathroom, studying herself in the mirror. Was that really her? Something seemed vastly different.

Her face looked worn and disheveled, hastily assembled. Two vertical furrows had been stamped into the space between her brows—an obvious weak spot that had split from the pressure of too many heavy burdens. Even the rest of her features seemed saggy and loose. Far too much wear and tear for a face that young.

But it wasn't that. She'd been aware for some time that she looked older than she was. Apparently being fearless made you age in dog years. So little time. So much suckage.

Was it the panic written into her expression? Her eyes did have that overly timid look, darting this way and that, as if constantly fleeing. And her lips were continually chapped from her biting them all the time.

No, it wasn't that either. Something else was changed—or missing. Something she couldn't quite pin down. She couldn't get past the question her reflection was begging of her.

What about D.? it asked. *How are you going to watch over D. if you can't take care of yourself?*

"Gaia?" Skyler rapped on the door, startling her. "Are you okay?"

"Y-Yeah," she replied, hopping back down. A warm tingle took shelter in her cheeks. She couldn't help feeling slightly embarrassed at having stared at herself for so long.

"You've been in there a long time," he called out. "Are you sick?"

Gaia hastily opened the door. "I'm fine," she said, trying to appear casual.

"Hey." He cupped her face in his hand and turned her gaze onto his. "I'm sorry about that lunatic. I know he really freaked you out."

The image of the ranting vagrant swam before her again. *Be thy brother's keeper.* . . . Her dread returned full force, gripping her like a lead straitjacket.

"Are you going to be okay?" Skyler's voice, forever full of concern, broke through her thoughts.

Was she? Was she ever going to be okay? She had no idea. But she wasn't sure she should say that. Part of her didn't want to worry him. After all, it was just Gaia the Melancholy, stewing in her own gloom and doom again. But she had to admit, part of her wanted to be comforted—to beg for a hug like a four-year-old with a skinned knee.

She swallowed back her panic and shrugged. "No big deal," she managed to whisper.

But of course, Skyler didn't buy it. She could tell by the swell of pity behind his eyes. "Come here." He pulled her to the couch and they sat down, Gaia nestling against him. "Listen, the city is full of crazy stuff. It's dangerous and cruel and relentless."

Gaia frowned. "Uh, Skyler? Is this supposed to be comforting?"

"Just hear me out." He squeezed her hand. "What I'm trying to say is that for me at least, things seem a lot less crazy when you're around. Forget the alley fight and the guy shouting nonsense at you. This has been one of the best days I've ever had."

She smiled. It really had been nice. Getting away from Collingwood, Jake, all the things that were complicating her already-hampered mind. For the first time since getting fear, she'd managed to relax, even if it was for just a little while. "Yeah," she replied. "Me too."

"When you're around, I just feel. . . I don't know. . . happier." He shook his head, grimacing slightly. "I know that sounds totally clichéd and cornball."

Gaia patted the top of his hand. "No," she said, glad for the chance to put him at ease for a change. "It doesn't."

He smiled crookedly. "I guess what I want to say is. . . I think we need each other. The world isn't going to stop being insane, and we can help each other out. I feel like we have this amazing connection, like I was meant to find you and look out for you. Am I nuts? Do you feel it, too?"

She paused, shifting her gaze to an abstract painting on the wall behind him. How did she feel? She couldn't tell. She'd been so completely petrified with fear for her brother that all other emotions were bound and gagged. But she had to admit there was something. Not since her mom died had there been someone so willing to watch over and protect her. In just one day Skyler had done so much for her, she wasn't even sure how to categorize him. Friend? Nurse? Big brother? Therapist? The attention he was giving her seemed so pure, so unconditional. It made her feel valued. And very, very grateful.

One thing was certain: she didn't want this to end. Skyler had been so incredible to her, she wasn't sure she could go back to doing everything for herself.

He was right. She obviously needed him. And now she was so beholden to him for his kindness, she would do whatever it took to somehow pay him back.

"Yes," she said finally. "I feel that way, too."

Skyler inhaled as if he'd been holding his breath, and his usual air of dignity returned to his features. "Good," he exclaimed. "Enough of all this." He stood and clapped. "What do you want to do tonight?"

Gaia tensed. Tonight? No. She had to get home. She had to contact D. and make sure he was all right.

"Uh. . . you know, I think I should probably head back to the boardinghouse."

His face fell. "But I thought you liked it here. I thought I was helping you get over all the stuff you've been through."

"You have. Really," she insisted, desperate to spare his feelings. "It's just that. . . if I stay away two nights in a row, Suko will probably freak. She won't buy the staying-at-a-girlfriend's-house excuse two nights in a row. And if she panics too much, she might even call my dad."

The more she lied and exaggerated, the more a mucky, greasy sensation spread over her. She was grotesque, awful. She should jump in the bathtub again and soak away the layer of crap she'd just dumped on herself. Wash away her sins.

Skyler didn't deserve this, but there was no way she could tell him about D. without unraveling the whole insane snarl that was her life.

"You're right," he said with a resigned nod. "I've kept you long enough."

He seemed so disappointed, Gaia was tempted to call the whole thing off and stay over again. And if it wasn't for the memory of D.'s innocent face haunting her every thought, she would have.

I'll make it up to you, Skyler, she thought as she slipped on her jacket. *Somehow.*

I have a term for this state I'm
in: *fearsickness*.

That has to be it. I've never
been carsick or airsick or hardly
even *sick* sick, but lately I just
feel. . . fearsick. Like I've
been poured over ice, splashed
with a jigger of fear, and shaken
until well blended. And my body
and mind haven't stopped spinning
yet.

I'm even afraid of being
afraid. My fear is so ever present that I can't remember what
it was like to be fearless. I do
recall that I was intensely
unhappy. That's what drove me to
have the procedure done in the
first place. But was it worse
than this? I just don't know.

I guess I thought that by getting the fear gene, I'd be gaining something. But instead it
feels more like I've lost something.

What? you ask.

Well, my sense of direction,
apparently. Ever since the first

wave of panic and terror hit my
nervous system, I've felt lost. I
still know my way around the
city, but I find the whole crushing, ominous sprawl of traffic
and buildings overwhelming. Even
sitting in a room with people is
disorienting. I find myself questioning every move I make or
phrase I utter, wondering how it
will make me look.

Also, I seem to have lost my
voice. My *inner* voice. You know?
That internal dialogue you have
with yourself that goes something
like, "Psychobabble, psychobabble, yadda, yadda, yadda"? In my
case it was more like, "Screw the
world. Who cares? Whatever.
Yadda, yadda, yadda."

Only that voice is quiet now.
It must have choked on fear and
died. All I hear in its place is
an uninterrupted whimpering. I
just don't know how to talk to
myself and make myself buy it.
It's a really lonely feeling.

So that's me. Aimless, hope-
less, and horrifically spineless.

I'm just a quivery globule of
fears. A booger beneath the bus
seat of life.

And now Skyler says he needs
me.

Weird.

He says we need each other—
that we were meant to be
together. And while I can definitely see how I've been benefit-
ing from our arrangement, I can't
see what he gets out of it. Maybe
he really feels this is part of
his destiny—that he was somehow
meant to find me.

The more I think about it, the
more I realize that no one else
in my life truly needs me. Not my
AWOL dad. Not Ed anymore. Not
Sam. Definitely not the FOHs.
Jake only needs the drama and
intrigue my life supplies. And
Loki would say he needs me, but
it's only as part of some grand,
malicious scheme.

Maybe no one has ever needed
me. I've been liked, perhaps even
loved at times, but never needed.
Now Skyler says he doesn't know

what he'd do without me. And I
have to admit, I don't know how
I've ever managed without him. We
do seem to need each other.
That's nice for a change.

I may not have a spine. But I
do still have a heart. In fact,
since fear came into my life,
it's been asserting itself more
than ever, squeezing and shudder-
ing within me like it's bruised
or cramped for space. The only
times I feel even vaguely normal
are when I'm with Skyler.

Right now Skyler is my voice,
my direction, my link to sanity.
And quite possibly my only anti-
dote for fearsickness.

GAIA SAT HALF CURLED IN THE
backseat of the world's
most repulsive cab. Its vinyl
upholstery seemed to be
coated in something slick. **Persephone**
The floorboards held a colorful, granular detritus that
also adhered to the greasy seat in places. Even the air
was clouded with an unpleasant scent—a weird
combination of fish sticks and Sanka.

And Skyler was there. Beside her. Skyler of private
limousines and expensive cars, who could probably
count the number of times he'd ridden in a cab on
one of his well-manicured hands.

She studied his Nordic profile as it appeared and
disappeared in the light of passing cars. Waves of guilt
spilled over her with every dip of the taxi, like cold
splashes of puddle water. "You know. . . you really
didn't have to ride home with me," she said.

His silhouette turned and the next illumination of
headlights revealed his off-center grin and reassuring
blue eyes. "I know. I wanted to come. No way was I
going to send you on your way alone after all you've
been through."

Gaia felt a corner of her mouth curl up to mirror
his. "Thanks," she whispered, snug in his gaze. The
guilt trickled away.

"I just wish you could have stayed," he added, facing front again.

And the guilt came back. Gaia chewed her lower lip and gazed out of her grime-streaked window. If only she could explain it to him. It wasn't that she didn't want to be with him; she just had to contact D. and make sure he was okay. Her encounter with the homeless man had dredged up an overwhelming fear for her brother's safety. But she had to keep all that from Skyler. Just for now.

As soon as enough time passed and her life fit some definition of normal, she would tell Skyler everything. She'd even introduce him to D. D. would love him. And she was sure Skyler would love D., maybe even want to take care of him, too.

In the meantime she just had to stay quiet and deal with her tides of guilt.

The strobe light effect of the oncoming traffic suddenly slowed. Gaia sat forward and glanced out of the slightly less dirty windshield. Sure enough, the Collingwood boardinghouse emerged from the hazy darkness. Gaia felt the familiar prick of dread, like a hypodermic to the gut.

"Now, see? Look at you," Skyler murmured as the cab pulled alongside the curb. "You're all tense again." He ran his hand through her hair. "I'm sorry I wasn't able to help you feel better."

Gaia whirled to face him. "But you did. I felt a lot better."

"But it didn't stick, did it?"

She looked down and shrugged.

"I'll miss you," he murmured, lifting her chin with his fingertips. "The apartment will seem big and lonely without you."

"I'll make it up to you," she said softly. "I promise."

"You know what? I know exactly how you can." Skyler tilted his head, a wry grin weighting his lopsided features. "You can spend the entire day with me tomorrow."

"But aren't you tired of me? Don't you need to—?"

He held up a hand, brushing her words aside. "Uh-uh. I won't take no for an answer. Unless. . ." He paused, looking slightly worried. "Do you have other plans?"

Plans? Gaia resisted the urge to snort ironically. *With my crowded social circle of admirers? All those wonderful people who left messages on my cell phone, wanting to make sure I was all right?*

"No," she said, barely audibly. Her tongue felt thick and limp with self-pity. "No plans."

"Good." Skyler leaned back, his arm resting jauntily along the top of the oily seat. "Here's what we'll do. I'll pick you up around eight tomorrow and take you out for breakfast. Then we'll have the rest of the day to goof off."

"Sounds great."

"You should probably wear good walking shoes. And dress comfortably but not too casually in case we want to eat someplace nice."

118

"Okay."

"Oh, and Gaia? Could you do something else for me?"

"Anything," she replied, eager for a chance to pay him back. "What is it?"

"Would you wear your hair down? I like it that way."

"Sure."

He beamed proudly at her, like a teacher rewarding his best student. Gaia drank it in. She'd never been a teacher's pet before, but she reveled in it now. She enjoyed Skyler's attention, felt both comforted and intoxicated by it. She'd do anything to keep getting those gold stars.

She opened the door and started to climb out of the cab.

"Gaia?"

"Yeah?" She turned back to face him and found. . . his face. He had slid across the grubby seat and was now occupying her airspace, tipping into her gravity. And suddenly and swiftly, like a magnet to steel, his lips locked onto hers.

A maelstrom of emotions surged forward. If Skyler's hands didn't have such a firm grip on her, she would have tumbled backward, through the door, onto the curb outside.

In the brief yet intense time she'd known Skyler, he'd kissed her many times. On her cheek, her forehead, her hair, her hand. Even a couple of pecks on the lips. But this. . . this wasn't a peck. It was too deep, too lingering. She knew there was a part of her that had always secretly wondered what it would be like to *really* kiss Skyler, that probably wanted to. But now, in his embrace, with his soft mouth pushing against hers, all she could focus on was the tangle of panicked thoughts jamming up her mind.

What did this mean? Was this serious or just a standard rich-boy goodbye picked up on his many jaunts to Europe? If it did mean something, was she enjoying it? Judging from her reciprocal lip action, she wasn't *not* enjoying it. But if she liked it, what about Jake? And why, oh why, couldn't she shut up her brain and go with it?

Bad fear gene! Bad! Bad!

And then, just like that, it was over. Skyler pulled away and settled back against the seat. "Good night," he murmured, smiling an uncategorical smile.

Gaia stumbled out into the crisp evening air. "Bye," she mumbled, still reeling from all the seismic emotional activity.

She shut the door and watched as the cab drove away, keeping her eyes on the curved shadow of Skyler's head. Eventually a delivery truck blocked it from view. Then she reached up and touched her fingers to her still-tingling lips.

That was some kiss! But what the hell did it mean? "Goodbye"? "Cheer up"? Or was it the start of something more intimate between her and Skyler?

No. She couldn't think about that now. Right now she had to focus on the mission at hand: checking on her beautiful, faraway brother. Once those fears had been put to rest, she could return to the mystery of the kiss.

Gaia turned and headed up the sidewalk. The brownstone looked more somber than usual in the pale yellow light of the streetlamps. It felt strange coming back, as if she'd been gone a long time. But this homecoming brought no sense of relief. In fact, every step toward it seemed to reverse Skyler's uplifting effects. She felt like Persephone, sent down to winter in Hades.

At least tomorrow she'd be with Skyler and it would be spring again. Even if just for one day.

From: gaia13@alloymail.com
To: dboy@shoalcreek.net
Re: Be careful!

Dearest D.,

Is everything all right with you? I know it's
been a few days since I last wrote and I'm sorry.
Please tell me everything is okay. Are you still
enjoying the farm? Is everyone still treating you
well?

If anything at all has gotten you down, let me
know. I don't know what I'd do if anything happened to you. Promise me you'll be careful.
Promise you'll tell me if anything upsets you.

I love you, D. Take care of yourself. Always
watch out for anything suspicious. You are so
innocent, you may not realize how dangerous and
insane a place the world can be. All we can do to
cope is to look out for each other.

I'm sorry I can't be there in person. I'll
join you again someday. Just stay safe and hang
on until I can get things straightened out here.

Love always,

Gaia

His body
language had
all the
characteristics
of someone

happy-ish

seriously
contemplating
self-
flagellation.

THE DOOR OPENED ONLY AS MUCH AS

the chain would allow. Through the crack Jake could see Suko's narrowed, disapproving eyes, focusing on Jake like two black missiles, ready to strike.

Perfectly Horrible

"Hello. Is Gaia here?" he asked, trying not to sound too eager. Suko had that all-knowing air about her. Her intense stare seemed almost capable of administering a long-range, wireless polygraph.

"It is eight-fifteen on a Sunday, very early to be visiting," she said reproachfully.

"Yes, I know. Sorry." No need to tell her that was the plan. Get here early before Gaia had a chance to slip through his fingers again. "If Gaia is still sleeping, I could wait outside on the porch until she wakes up."

"She is not here."

"What?" Jake shouted. Stern furrows erupted around Suko's eyes and mouth. "I'm sorry," he added, returning to a meek, Beaver Cleaver tone, "I just don't understand why she wouldn't be here. Did she not come home last night either?"

"She came home."

He waited for further elaboration. When none came, he asked, "Did she get my message? I told Zan to tell her to call."

"You will have to ask Zan."

Again he waited, staring at her scowl through the narrow rectangular opening. "So. . . could I talk to Zan?"

"She's sleeping."

Jake reached up and grasped a handful of his spiky, unwashed hair. "Can I ask," he began, carefully blockading his frustration, "where Gaia is now?"

"She is not here. She left at eight o'clock."

Damn! He'd just missed her! After thirty-six hours of frantic searching, he'd come within fifteen minutes of meeting her face-to-face. He'd lost Gaia *twice*.

He almost wished he hadn't come so close. He almost wished Suko had said she'd never come home—*almost*.

"You should leave now. As I said, you are here too early. Also, you should know that you are not allowed to visit her here."

"Look," he said, opening his arms in a gesture of surrender, "couldn't I just wait here for her?"

"No. Now please leave." Suko nodded toward the sidewalk, a s h a r d o f a n g e r in her typically smooth tone.

"What if I just waited until Zan wakes up and asked her some questions?"

"No!" Suko hit a volume level Jake hadn't thought her capable of. He got the distinct feeling few people had ever heard it—or lived to talk about it. "If you do not leave now, I will call 911! Do you understand?"

"Yes," he said with a resigned sigh. "Sorry."

But Suko had already shut the door. Jake could see the nearby curtains flutter. Her sharp black eyes appeared in a corner of the front window, watching him.

I'm going. I'm going. He loped down the front path, beaten and disgraced, like a mangy dog that had strayed onto Suko's well-kept lawn. If he'd had a tail, it would have been tucked between the legs of his faded blue Levi's.

So it was official. Gaia was definitely ignoring him. She had returned home and didn't even bother to call. At this point she must have gotten the six or seven messages he'd left on her cell phone or at least heard from Zan that he'd stopped by. Obviously she had no desire to talk to him.

If it was only a cold-shoulder treatment, that would be one thing. Jake could handle a brush-off. But he knew it was much worse than that. Gaia was in trouble. Oliver sure sensed it, and even he—lamest of all investigators—sensed it, too.

Jake ambled down the block until he was certain he was out of Suko's monitoring range. He leaned against a brick wall surrounding a small park and playground and closed his eyes, feeling simultaneously restless and weary.

Where to now? Where could Gaia have gone so early?

A sudden, pulsating sensation emanated from the

left side of his waist. Jake jumped sideways and pawed at the throbbing area. His hands closed around the boxy, alphanumeric pager clipped to his pants. A loan from Oliver.

Jake hit the display button and read Oliver's brief, irritable-looking message:

Report in.

Beautiful. Now he had to go face the man he admired above all others and admit that he was a total failure. The perfect cap to this `perfectly horrible` weekend.

GAIA STARED AT SKYLER AS HE STOOD

Sherpa in the subway aisle, rocking sideways with the rhythmic motion of the train. Just like in the cab the night before, Gaia noticed he looked out of place among all the other subway riders. A descended demigod among mere mortals.

It wasn't just his custom-made shirt or his sharp, patrician profile. Nor did it have to do with that über-confident, almost overly erect way he stood. It was something more. . . metaphysical.

Skyler Rodke, Gaia noticed, had an unmistakable energy that extended beyond his corporeal borders. At times she imagined she could see it gathering, nimbuslike, around him. It was evident in the way his blond hair seemed to give off its own light, in the way his blue eyes flickered like gas jets, and in the magnetic tug she felt in his presence. He was a walking power source. A gas giant who had pulled her into his orbit.

She wasn't the only one who sensed it, either. As they moved through the subway, she'd watched the other riders instinctively make way for him, like peasants for a passing king.

Gaia wondered if by being around him, she could absorb some of that energy, increase her own stores of confidence. She had to admit it was already working. Whenever she was with Skyler, she didn't feel quite so adrift. And then there was that kiss. . . .

Even if it hadn't meant something bigger than friendship was brewing between them, it had been beautifully meaningful—a physical manifestation of the incredible connection they shared. She now knew that his feelings for her matched the depths she felt for him, whatever those emotions happened to be.

Skyler caught her staring at him and smiled. She smiled back, blushing slightly, then stared out the window into the dark tunnel. She still wasn't bold enough to meet his eyes for long.

"You ready for breakfast?" he asked.

Gaia shrugged. "Sure."

"I know a great place. I'll take you there."

The subway was slowing down, and people were pressing in around them, making for the exit. Skyler pointed to the doors, as if indicating that this was to be their stop. Gaia slipped her bag over her shoulder, holding tight to the strap, and joined the traffic jam of people.

As soon as the glass-and-metal doors opened, Gaia was bounced in every direction. It suddenly seemed like the entire train was disembarking. As the people surged forward, she kept her eye out for Skyler's white blond hair but couldn't see him anywhere. Had he already gotten off? Or was this not the right stop after all?

Eventually she reached the exit. She stood in the doorway, scanning the train platform for Skyler as more people pushed past her, getting on and off, a few yelling at her to move out of the way. But there was still no sign of him.

Gaia frowned. Should she go back and check the subway car? Or should she get off? *Don't panic,* she told herself. She didn't want to spin out of control again. Not here. Not without Skyler.

"Hey, Gaia!"

She glanced in the direction of the voice. The crowd was dispersing, hurrying toward the street exits, and Skyler was becoming visible near the front of the platform.

"Over here!" he shouted as he jogged toward her, waving his left arm as if directing a 747 toward the runway.

Just then the train hissed loudly, releasing its brakes. As Gaia made to step onto the platform, the door snapped shut. Its thick rubber edges closed around her bag, wrenching her right arm backward. She scrambled about, pulling as hard as she could to free herself, but with one arm effectively tied to the train, she couldn't get up enough leverage.

Finally, by pushing her left leg against the side of the train, she managed to squirm back and forth, tugging her bag out from between the rubber grips. Little by little she could feel the strap give way until the bag popped out from between the doors, freeing her.

The force sent her forward into Skyler's waiting arms, and they tumbled back onto the concrete platform in a heap. A second later the train pulled away in a tirade of hisses and squeaks.

"Good catch," she said, laughing nervously.

Skyler sat up and grasped her hands, pulling them both to their feet. "Are you hurt?" he asked, looking her over.

"No." She rubbed her shoulder distractedly. "Not really. I'm just. . . in shock, I guess." She stared over at the now-empty track, dizzy with disbelief. She hated to think what would be happening to her right now if she hadn't gotten loose. Would anyone have noticed?

Or would they have found her at the next stop, splattered all over the glass doors like some overgrown insect?

"Yeah, you must be pretty freaked," Skyler said, throwing his arm around her and guiding her toward the staircase. "Come on. Let's go."

"Hey, Skyler."

He paused and looked at her. "What? What's wrong?"

"Nothing, just. . . thanks for being here."

He smiled magnificently. "My pleasure."

Gaia settled into his half embrace and let him maneuver her through the crowd.

She liked this feeling, having someone at her side, her very own Sherpa guiding her through the treacherous city. It was a feeling she could get used to. Real fast.

LOKI WAS STANDING IN FRONT OF

Mummified

his window, meditatively rolling a coin in his left hand, when suddenly he heard his front door buzzer.

It was surely Jake. He could almost tell by the way he buzzed—weak and fitful, like the drone of a dying mosquito.

As Loki undid the bolts on his door, affixing a calm, questioning expression onto his features, he concluded that things had not gone according to plan. Jake would have surely contacted him with news of any success, eager for his pat on the head. The fact that he had not heard from the boy since sending him on his mission could only mean trouble.

Had Gaia argued with him? Had she been restrained in some way? He had much to ask. Even small details Jake would consider unimportant could provide them with the most valuable clues.

He undid the final bolt and pulled open the door. Jake leaned against the frame, looking bent and shriveled, almost `mummified with guilt`. His body language had all the characteristics of someone seriously contemplating self-flagellation.

This could be worse than I thought, Loki worried.

"Jake," he greeted warmly, pulling the door wider. "Come in. Sit down. Would you like something to drink?"

"No. Thank you." Jake dragged himself across the room and dropped into a leather armchair, slouching so far down, his long legs barely bent.

Loki took the chair across from him. He sat back casually and smiled at Jake, taking in the boy's rumpled shirt and unkempt hair, not to mention the lawn of whiskers across his cheeks. "So. . . ," he began, "what sorts of things have you found out about my niece?"

Jake closed his eyes. A faint line appeared on his forehead, cleaving it in two. "Nothing," he said almost noiselessly.

Loki steadied his breathing before speaking again. "What do you mean by 'nothing'?"

"Exactly that," Jake mumbled, meeting Loki's gaze. "Nothing. I haven't even seen Gaia since I left you. I couldn't find her."

"You *what*?" Loki growled, sitting forward in his armchair, ready to pounce. His right hand opened and shut reflexively, as if grasping for a weapon.

Stupid infant! Amateur! He'd been a fool to place any faith in the boy. It was one thing to have failed to reason with Gaia—he himself had stumbled in that regard. But to let her remain out of their sight for almost two days? That was inexcusable.

By now anything could have happened to her. Judging by her actions before disappearing, she'd been in a most vulnerable state. She would have been Silly Putty in the hands of someone skilled enough to exploit her.

Jake had tensed considerably, his limbs bending inward in a protective stance. He watched Loki warily with sunken eyes.

Enough, Loki scolded himself. He shouldn't risk scaring the boy, even if he was a useless pile of tissue and testosterone. He had to keep him on his side in case there was still a chance of getting through to Gaia.

He hastily transformed his features into those of a stricken uncle. "I've just been so worried," he agonized, holding his head in his hands. "After so long. . . you'd think there would be some breakthrough."

"I'm sorry, Oliver," Jake said morosely. He heaved a great sigh and sank back defeatedly into the chair cushions. "I tried everything. Skyler doesn't live on campus, and I couldn't get his address from any records or his family."

"Do you mean she's still with this. . . *person*?" Loki continued to restrain himself.

"I—I don't know. I know she went back to the boardinghouse last night, but she left early this morning. She could be anywhere, with anyone."

Jake's whining was becoming wearisome. Loki didn't have the time or the patience to bolster the boy's confidence. He could only continue to gnaw at his pride, in the hopes that it would spring back to life. "So you've given up?"

"No!" Jake cried. "I mean, not really. It's just. . . what am I supposed to do? I've already tried everything."

"No, you haven't," Loki said calmly. "You are simply not working hard enough. You might have tried everything that first came to mind, but that's not everything. There are always ways to get what you want—if you think of them."

"Right," Jake muttered. Loki could see him waver, see his ego gradually seeping back in his posture. All he needed was one final push.

"No," he said with a sigh. "Perhaps I should apologize to you. Maybe I was wrong to send you on this mission. You're young. And you're close to Gaia. I can see how you might instinctively want to spare yourself any more frustration. Perhaps I should bring in someone else." He stood and headed for his desk, waiting for Jake to stop him. It was a daring bluff. There was no one else he could call.

Sure enough, before he even reached the spot where the desk's shadow slanted forward along the stained concrete floor, Jake was back on his feet. "Stop," he called out. "I can do it! I promise."

Loki turned and pretended to be regarding him. "Are you sure? This is very vital. Gaia could be in even more danger than you or I realize. It's important that we act fast."

"I know," Jake assured him, his chin raised and his jaw set. Loki was glad to see that tough swagger reasserting itself. Boys like Jake were so predictable.

Jake paced in a small arc, his left hand massaging his right fist. "Don't worry, Oliver," he said. "I have a plan. A good one."

"Excellent," Loki replied. *I hope that you do, Mr. Montone. For your sake, I sincerely hope that you do.*

GAIA TWIRLED HER FORK COUNTER-

clockwise, making five concentric swirly patterns on her plate. The eggs Skyler had ordered for her had been vivisected enough to look like a few bites were missing, but the truth was, she still hadn't gotten up the nerve to try them. When they'd arrived, she'd been horrified by the mass of sauce covering the poached eggs—a gloppy, snot-colored substance interspersed with chunks of mossy green spinach.

At least the potato pancakes that came with it had been delicious. And the coffee was great, too—a strong European blend that had dispelled the last foggy remnants of sleep from her body. Now if she could just get rid of the rest of this grossness. . .

"What's wrong?" Skyler's voice cut through her thoughts. "Don't you like your eggs Florentine?"

"Sure," Gaia lied. "I was just spacing out." She held her breath and shoveled in a large spoonful, aiming for the rear of her mouth to avoid as many taste buds as possible. It flopped on the back of her tongue for a few seconds before sliding down her throat. "*Mmm.*"

The fact that she couldn't stand the stuff was only further proof that she didn't know anything. After all, this was one of those trendy bistros that had a chef instead of a fry cook. How could someone like her, who considered a bowl of Froot Loops to be high-class breakfast dining, even begin to appreciate the finer stuff?

"So what were you thinking about?" Skyler asked.

"Stuff." She knew that wasn't a good enough answer, but she didn't want to lie or risk insulting him with the truth: that she'd been formulating a plan to dump the contents of her plate into the nearby potted palm.

"Like what? Is anything worrying you?"

She thought of D. She'd checked her e-mail that morning, but he hadn't written her back yet. And calling him wasn't really an option. . . D. just wasn't built for talking on the phone. "Just. . . family stuff."

He looked at her pityingly. "You must really miss your dad, huh?"

She shrugged. "Sometimes."

"Forgive me for saying this, but how can he just leave you like this for long periods?"

"He doesn't want to. It's just part of the job."

"I think it's stupid that you have to stay in that depressing boardinghouse. I mean, why not live on your own? Or with a friend? With me?"

Gaia blinked up at him in surprise. Did he just mention her living with him? Skyler's features contained no hint of irony. He stared back at her, perfectly placid, waiting for her reply. "I guess my dad just thought I'd be safer there," she replied.

"That's bull. My building is safe. I could keep you safe. Don't I always look out for you?"

"Yes. You do. But my dad doesn't know you. And he'd probably wonder—" She cut herself off, swallowing the words *what's going on between us.*

Don't go there, she told herself, staring down at her plate. Kiss or not, she didn't want to analyze what she had with Skyler. Something this intense had no real category anyway. It was special. It was hers. If she sliced it and diced it and placed it under a microscope, she could risk ruining it forever.

Skyler leaned across the table. "Don't you ever get lonely?" he asked softly.

Gaia's head snapped up. "What?"

"I just feel bad for you being alone like that. You should be with family, people who love you, look out for you. Your dad's missing out on so much."

A cold sensation spilled through Gaia's chest. She glanced back down and began trolling her fork through the gelatinous goo, churning up chunks of spinach. Skyler seemed to be doing this exact thing to her mind—sifting through and extracting all her deeply buried frustrations. She realized she still hated her father for leaving her like this, even if she did understand it. "It's not his fault," she said, to herself as well as Skyler. "He can't help it."

"Can't he?" Skyler set down his fork and leaned back against the wrought iron chair. "I mean, hasn't he ever considered switching careers so he can spend more time with you?"

138

Gaia didn't reply. She threw down her fork and pushed her dish aside. Why *hadn't* her father ever thought about quitting? Was it because of Loki? Was it out of some overwhelming sense of patriotic duty?

Or did he just prefer being on the job to being with her?

Skyler reached forward and grasped her hand. "Sorry," he said. "I know it's none of my business. I just want to see you happy. That's all."

"I know," she said, managing a brave smile.

"What do you say we get out of here?"

Gaia watched Skyler pay the check and marveled at his sharp instincts. Had the two of them lingered at their table for even a moment longer, Gaia might well have slipped into a deep funk. For a keen awareness of the lameness of her life had just begun to seep over her like warm tar. The mother who'd been murdered, the father who was constantly on the run, the brother no one else knew about, hidden away on an Iowa farm, possibly in danger, the grandfather and cousins locked up for unspeakable crimes, and finally, the only close-by relative, *her whack-job uncle*, all pretty much amounted to a family life worthy of shame. But Skyler's perfectly timed suggestion to leave was just the nudge she needed to get her mind off herself and onto more uplifting subjects. Like Skyler.

Or rather, how good Skyler was for her.

GAIA WAS FEELING AS CLOSE TO HAPPY

Alarm Bells

as she had since her genetic transformation. It was a comfortable sensation, not bliss or even true contentment, but a nice, easy equilibrium. She was happy-*ish*. Happy-*esque*. The weather was sunny and breezy. Her shoulder had stopped throbbing from her earlier run-in with the subway doors. And as she walked through the relative Sunday quiet of the Garment District with Skyler, she couldn't help feeling like she was making peace with the city.

They were making their way across Seventy-sixth Street toward Madison Avenue, peering into the boutiques and occasionally laughing at some of the more outlandish fashions—the feathered blouse, the jacket with puffy, balloon-shaped sleeves, the hats as large as microwave ovens.

"Check out that one." Gaia pointed to a round red monstrosity that resembled a latticework sombrero. "That's definitely one for the boardroom, huh?"

"Yeah," Skyler said with a laugh. "Wise business move. Sell clothing that will trap your customers in revolving doors."

"Spoken like a future CEO," Gaia said, raising her Starbucks cappuccino toward him. "I mean, that *is* the plan, right? You're studying business in order to take over your dad's company?"

"I guess," he said, shrugging and glancing skyward. "I haven't really decided yet."

She nodded solemnly. Together they turned away from the shop window and resumed strolling down the street.

It was obvious Skyler didn't like talking about himself, which was ironic since she felt obligated to turn the topic of conversation onto him after he'd shown so much interest in her. She should probably just lay off, though. College was surely stressful, and he no doubt had family pressures she couldn't begin to fathom. Still, she couldn't help but be a little bothered by the fact that their friendship was so out of balance. All she wanted was to get to know him better, maybe even offer advice on something, the way he always did for her.

The shops seemed to be getting more expensive and formal as they continued walking. Eventually they found themselves in front of a swanky dress shop with a row of headless mannequins in the window. Each one was draped in a shiny or sequined formal gown, and the floor was strewn about with CDs of teen pop idols like Britney and Justin and Pink to indicate that the dresses were intended for prom.

Gaia leaned her forehead against the window, staring at the display. Alarm bells bonged through her brain, nagging her about what little time she had left until the "big night." She should really decide on a dress and soon. Only. . . the last time she'd chosen a fancy designer dress, she'd had Liz Rodke, the supreme fashionista herself, as her private personal shopper. There was no way Gaia could brave it on her own.

Ask Skyler, came a voice in her head over all the distress signals.

She stepped back and studied Skyler's reflection in the window glass. Perfect. He always seemed to know what was good for her. Besides, the guy was probably born in formal wear. He'd be the perfect consultant.

"You all right?" Skyler asked, for roughly the forty-sixth time since emerging from the subway. It was thoughtful but also an eensy bit annoying.

"I'm fine," she replied, her breath fogging the glass. "I was just thinking."

"About prom?"

She turned and gaped at him. "How did you know?"

He smiled mysteriously and took a long, noisy sip from his plastic foam coffee cup. "I can guess," he said eventually. "Wasn't that long since I was in high school. I know about such things."

She turned back to the boutique's display window, trying to picture her head on any of them. Would black be appropriate? Would the snug purple one be flattering or too hootchie mama?

Of course. . . technically she hadn't even been asked yet. Was Jake ever going to get around to that? Did he not realize that prom required a level of planning typically found only in the Pentagon? Or maybe he didn't want to go to prom. Or just didn't want to go with her.

"So who are you going with?" Skyler asked. Again he seemed to be expertly scanning her thoughts.

"I don't know. Probably Jake."

"The Italian Stallion?" He snorted. "You're kidding."

"What's wrong with that?" she asked, feeling slightly offended.

"He isn't good enough for you. I'm sorry, I know this isn't my business, but prom is supposed to be one of those personally historic moments. And he doesn't know how to treat you. Why waste a special evening on an insensitive goon like him?"

Gaia fiddled with the wrapper on her coffee cup. All the frustration and hurt feelings she had for Jake were suddenly jostling toward the forefront. It was true he was taking his own sweet time about asking her, and he had been giving her the silent treatment this weekend. Plus there was the Oliver worship. But did any of that mean she should give up on him? Skyler was being a little overly judgmental. *Or*—she suddenly thought of his kiss the night before—*could he be jealous?*

"Well, it's not like I have lots of options," she said, peeling off the Starbucks label in a long thin spiral. "I mean, technically Jake *is* my boyfriend."

"If that's true"—Skyler stepped forward, compelling

her to look up at him—"why did you come to *me* after that fight instead of him?"

Gaia turned away, crushing her cup in her fist. She couldn't answer that. Because, frankly, she had no answer.

Skyler made an irritatingly good point. She *hadn't* wanted Jake that time. Maybe fear had given her some new `animal-like instincts`. Maybe all this time her body had been telling her what her mind wouldn't.

Was it over between her and Jake?

His embrace
was extremely
tight, almost
frantic—the
type of hug
you'd **urgency**
give
someone
heading off
to prison.

"ARE YOU SURE YOU DON'T WANT

to hang out a little while longer?" Skyler asked with a nod toward downtown. They were standing next to a news- **Tapeworm** stand on Bleecker and Charles Street, only a few blocks from the boardinghouse. Gaia couldn't believe how late it was. Darkness had come unnaturally fast, as if someone had hit a gigantic off switch.

"I really can't," she replied, smiling apologetically. "I almost missed curfew last night and Suko has her radar on me. If I come home late, there'll be hell to pay. I still think she has a room somewhere in the house that's full of medieval torture devices."

Skyler laughed. "Wouldn't be surprised. Still, I hate to end this. I've had so much fun." He grabbed her hand and pulled it up, studying it under the lamplight.

"Me too," she replied. It had been a pretty good day overall. Skyler had planned the whole thing to perfection. He had shown her all his favorite hangouts. The kooky bookstore in the West Village. The combination music shop and café on Fifty-eighth. It had all been so nice and simple. In spite of a few confusing moments, she felt really close to Skyler and immensely grateful for his guidance.

She stared down at her long, tapered fingers clasped within his thicker, sturdier ones. The dim lavender glow from the streetlight cast everything into soft focus, making it hard to see where her hand ended and his began—almost as if they'd been fused together.

"Well, let's go, then," he said with a resigned sigh. "You have school tomorrow."

School. The word fell into her gut like a cannonball. Jake would be there. The FOHs. All the people she didn't have the heart or energy to see.

Suddenly she wanted Skyler to hold her hand forever, to lead her around and tell her what to do and what to think. Things were so much simpler with him around. With him she felt like she could handle anything. She felt almost. . . fearless.

Just then he let go. "Come on," he said, charging across the street. "Before the light changes."

Gaia looked down at her empty hand. It felt strange, almost incomplete. After a weekend in Skyler's care, she didn't want to go back to doing things alone. She wasn't sure she could handle it. She'd have no guidance, no source of strength—a tapeworm without a host.

"Gaia!"

Skyler's voice snapped her from her gloom. He was standing in the center of the street, beckoning to her. Trancelike, Gaia stepped off the curb and followed him.

Beep! Beeeeeeep!

She was only four steps away from joining Skyler on the center stripe when a taxicab careened around the corner, blaring its horn. There came a rush of light, noise, and movement. Her muscles seemed to spring in all directions. She saw the blinding headlights, heard the crunch of the tires against the asphalt, and felt her hip slide against the sharp contour of the front panel. Then Skyler was there, his strong arms pulling her toward him as the taxi sped away in a spray of smoke and diesel fumes.

"Idiot!" he yelled after the cab as they hobbled in their clumsy embrace toward the other side of the street.

Gaia stared at him. It was becoming her nightmare, the Scary Skyler image she'd seen after her fight in the alley and her freaky encounter with the vagrant. His face was a series of crisscrossed lines, and blue veins stood out on his forehead. There was no trace of his easygoing, regal spirit. His rage was almost primal, not unlike a pit bull's.

"It's okay. I'm fine," she said, craning her head to meet his eyes and calm him down. "It was my fault, really. I wasn't looking where I was going."

"No. He was going way too fast. Man, I hate people like that!" He looked at her finally, his expression softening. "I'm just glad I was there to grab you."

"Yep. That's you," she said, grinning nervously. "My own personal superhero."

Skyler gave her a reassuring hug. Then they linked hands and continued toward the boardinghouse. *See,* she told herself. *No biggie. Scary Skyler only emerges when he thinks you're in danger. He's just protective— not scary.*

"I've said this before, and I mean it," he said, giving her hand a squeeze. "The city is a dangerous place. We've got to always look out for each other."

"Right," she replied with a solemn nod.

They walked in silence the rest of the way. Skyler's words sank into her, making her think of poor, innocent D. He had to have read her e-mail by now. Maybe he'd written her back? At last she had something to look forward to back at Collingwood.

Soon they were standing on the sidewalk in front of the tall brownstone. Obviously people were still up. Pale yellow light shone from beneath the shades of two windows above the front stoop, reminding her of two heavily lidded eyes and a gaping mouth.

"Here you are," Skyler announced, as if this had been Gaia's main destination all along. As if she couldn't wait to go in and get swallowed up by the house.

"Yeah. Home sweet home," she said glumly.

"It's not too late to change your mind." He raised his brows expectantly.

"No. I can't risk a major Suko freak-out. She'd probably get my dad, the cops, and the mayor on my ass."

"Fine. But I wish you didn't have to stay here," he said, giving the house a dirty look.

"We'll see each other again soon," Gaia said. She felt anxious to please him. Somehow she sensed that her refusal to stay out longer upset him, even if he said he understood.

"How about tomorrow?" he suggested. "I can meet you after school."

School. There was that word again. Gaia's stomach seemed to be on a plummeting freight elevator. But then. . . if she had Skyler to look forward to, maybe it would be enough to get her through the day?

"Sounds perfect," she said. "I'll meet you out front."

Skyler stepped forward and Gaia braced herself for another prolonged kiss. This time she wouldn't be taken off guard. This time she would focus on what was there and figure out how she really felt.

Only this time Skyler opened his arms and pulled her into a hug. "Good night," he murmured.

Gaia felt somewhat let down. She'd wanted it to happen again—if only to analyze it. She waited to see if the cuddling evolved into something more, but he just kept holding her close. Yet his embrace was extremely tight, almost frantic—the type of hug you'd give someone heading off to prison.

"Sleep well, okay?" he whispered in her ear. "I

really hate leaving you here." His pity seemed to pass through to her, making her feel even more miserable.

"I will," she replied, pulling away.

She turned and walked toward the house, hating it more with every step. Skyler was right. She didn't belong here. What exactly was she returning to, anyway? Just a few worldly possessions and, hopefully, an e-mail from her brother. That was it.

This wasn't a home. It was an oversized locker. Maybe she should move out.

At the door she turned and waved to Skyler. He lifted his hand and then started off down the block, vanishing into the shadows.

Gaia stepped inside, glancing about in case Suko was waiting with one of her hypercritical stares. But no one was downstairs. As quietly as she could, she crept up the creaky staircase and into her bedroom.

There is *a god,* she thought as she shut the door with a satisfying click. Now she could check for D.'s e-mail in peace.

She reached over and turned on the light. Then suddenly, as if the switch had triggered some inner mechanism of her own, she spun around and raised her hands in a fighting stance.

Someone was there. She had seen them out of the corner of her eye, crouched in the nook beyond her bed. And that someone was rising up and heading right for her.

"GAIA."

Jake was so glad to see her. He had an overwhelming urge to scoop her up and hold her close, reversing the effects of those long hours of worry.

Wounded Pride

But she remained in her attack stance, a variety of expressions playing over her face. "What the hell are you doing here?" she said finally.

"I had to see you. I've been looking everywhere."

Gaia lowered her hands, but still she didn't approach him. Her eyes tapered into narrow slits, regarding him coolly. "And you thought breaking into my room would be the best approach?"

"It was the only way," he said, plopping onto her bed. "Suko wasn't about to let me through the door. I just had to see you and make sure you were all right."

"I'm *fine*," she snapped.

"Right. Good." Jake was completely thrown by her hostile tone. After all, *he* wasn't the one who'd stayed over at someone else's house. *He* hadn't ignored countless phone messages.

Stay cool. Get a grip. He tried to remember why he was there, the urgency of his mission. "I have something important to tell you. To warn you about."

"What is it?" she asked, softening only slightly.

"We think Skyler Rodke might be behind some of this bad stuff that's been happening to you."

Gaia's features gaped wide with surprise, then gradually froze over. "Oh, really? *We* think that, do we? By 'we' do you mean you and your new best friend, Loki?"

"It's Oliver!" he shouted. "And yes. He has good reasons for being suspicious."

"Well, whatever he thinks, he's wrong."

"Gaia, listen," he began slowly. He shifted on the bed, searching her eyes for any sign of logical thought. "I went over to the Rodkes' a couple of nights ago, looking for you. While I was there, I found your hair elastic—the one those IV heads pulled off you during the fight."

"Christ, that could be anyone's. That doesn't prove a thing."

He shook his head. "You can't take that chance. You've got to stay away from Skyler—maybe all the Rodkes."

"Why?" she argued, her voice rising. "Skyler has been nothing but good to me all this time, and now you accuse him of some sort of scheming? Based on what? A *rubber band?* Do you realize how stupid that sounds? He actually cares about me. He looks out for me and makes sure I'm okay—unlike some people who never call."

"I *did* call," Jake cried, jumping up from the bed. "I called half a dozen times! I even came by and—"

153

"Spare me!" she hissed, giving a sardonic jerk of her head. "I don't want to hear any more of your lies. If anyone's been doing some scheming against me, it's you and that freak uncle of mine!"

Jake was stunned by the intensity of her wrath. He could barely recognize her rutted, red-streaked face. In the time he'd known her, he'd seen a wide collection of angry looks on Gaia's face, but this was by far the worst.

"Gaia, calm down. Will you just listen for a minute?" He paused, waiting in case she went off on him again. But she just stood there, quietly glaring at him. "You have to admit there could be a connection," he went on. "Think about it. All the trouble with the IV heads? It started when the Rodkes came to town. And now the hair band just happens to turn up at their house? It's too much to be coincidence. Skyler could be—"

"*Shut up!*" she shouted.

Jake stared at her in mute horror. Her eyes were wide and wild, and her entire body looked tense, almost like she wanted to hit him. Seeing her so unbalanced was at once jarring and tragic and strangely ominous. In the long, squirming moment that followed, he considered whether it would be both feasible and advisable to grab Gaia in a half nelson and wrestle her into a straitjacket.

"Now you listen to me," Gaia continued. Her voice

was lowered but her fists were still clenched tight. "Skyler is amazing. He *needs* me—unlike you. All you ever wanted from me was getting a thrill off my crazy, danger-filled life. And now you're teaming up with Loki, trying to freak me out even more, just so you can play spy! Well, guess what? It's not going to work. I'll never turn on Skyler. In fact. . . I'm going to prom with him."

"What?" Something was horribly wrong here. He was worried sick about her safety and she was babbling on about prom? At what point did things go from all-out whack job to completely incomprehensible?

"That's right. So really, there's no reason for us to be together anymore. We're through. Finished. Cremated. Go find some other girl to play mind games with."

"Gaia," he said softly, reaching out for her. He had never meant for it to get this bad between them. He knew he'd screwed up. He'd been anxious, mad, full of wounded pride. He'd forgotten his promise to listen to her.

"Get off!" she spat, shrinking back from his arms. "I mean it! If you don't get out of here right now, I'll scream for Suko."

Jake stepped back, scanning her face for irony or guilt, but there was none. He had no doubt she'd make good on her threat. And having already been threatened by Suko to have the cops sicced on him, he really didn't want to risk another tangle with her.

He held Gaia's gaze a few seconds longer and then turned away. Walking over to the window, he threw his legs over the sill and scooted along the narrow ledge to the nearby trellis. Then he slowly climbed down, keeping his eyes on Gaia as she watched from the window.

Funny. For days he'd been praying just to see her. He figured if he had the chance to talk to her, he could reason with her, get her to understand the danger she might be in.

Now he'd gotten his wish. He'd seen her. He'd talked with her. He'd delivered his warning. And now he was more worried than ever.

Because the one thing he hadn't thought possible had actually happened—Gaia Moore had completely lost her grip.

GAIA FELT A TUG AS SHE WATCHED

Jake lope dejectedly into the night. Was it remorse? No. She was way too angry for that. It was more like. . . a shallow grief. Like the nostalgia one got tossing out a favorite pair of jeans: lots of

Little Bitty Test

good times, could have been more, but there were way too many rips to be mended.

Served him right, she told herself, turning away from the sill. She'd been out of her mind with anger. She probably shouldn't have lied about going to prom with Skyler, but she couldn't stand to hear the crazy things Jake was saying about him.

Skyler had been so right. The guy was just a macho thrill seeker. Only a true sicko would jump out of a dark corner like that, trying to freak her out.

Yet. . . A sudden realization swept over her, like an overly aggressive heat rash. . . . *She hadn't been scared at all.* She'd come home to find someone lurking in her room and hadn't been the least bit afraid!

Gaia slowly replayed the episode in her mind. It was true. She'd been angry with him for using such a stupid, Loki-like tactic. And she was still sore at him for not calling the past couple of days. But there wasn't the slightest hint of fear. Not a single skipped heartbeat.

"Wait a minute," she whispered, grabbing ahold of the bedpost. "It's been longer than that."

Closing her eyes, she mentally skimmed over the events of the day. The subway doors catching her arm had been frustrating, but it hadn't made her pulse race. And when the cab careened around the corner, Skyler assumed he'd saved her in the nick of time. But really, it was her own quick reaction that made her sidestep the car—Skyler only yanked her out of the way a second *after* she'd avoided getting hit. If she'd been frozen by fear, she would have been run over for sure. Come to think of it, she hadn't experienced a trace of fear all day.

What happened to my fear? she wondered. *Is it fading? Is it gone?*

There was one way to know for sure. Gaia grabbed a jacket off her desk chair and quickly pulled it on.

Wait, no. She paused in the middle of zipping up. This was stupid. She could be making a huge, dangerous mistake.

But then, she had to know, didn't she? She owed it to herself to find out what was happening to her.

Okay. She'd do it. She headed over to her open window and swung her legs over the sill.

She'd just check it out for a while. Nothing crazy. Just a little bitty test.

From: megan21@alloymail.com
To: shred@alloymail.com
Re: promstuff

Hey! I heard you asked Kai to prom. You guys are too, too cute! Looks like everyone is paired up. Well, *almost* everyone. I guess you heard what Gaia did to poor Jake. What a shock, huh? You were smart to break up with her when you did. I would hate to think of her doing something like that to you.

From: megan21@alloymail.com
To: heatherg@alloymail.com
Re: Warning

Hey, girl! How are you?

Just wanted to keep you up to date on what's been going on here. . . Listen, I know I know she's your friend and all and that you guys have been keeping in touch while you've been away, but you need to hear what sort of things Gaia is up to. I know it's probably none of my business, but I'm only concerned about you.

Gaia is up to her wicked, wicked ways again. She totally cheated on Jake with Skyler Rodke. I'm serious. The girl obviously has a major ego problem when it comes to men.

I'm only telling you this for your own good. She has major loyalty issues—if she can't stay true to her boyfriends, then she probably can't stay true to her girlfriends, either.

From: megan21@alloymail.com
To: jakem@alloymail.com
Re: Moving on

Hey. I just wanted to say that I'm sooo sorry about what Gaia did to you. None of us can believe she would stoop this low. You deserve better and you know it.

So have you ever considered asking Laura out?

This was
what she was
meant to do.
She knew it
with **mother**
every
hormonally **ship**
charged
molecule in
her being.

Technicolor Fantasies

ED SAT AT HIS DESK, FROWNING AT his computer screen as if challenging it to a duel. Since when did Megan send him e-mails? And what did she mean about Gaia doing something to Jake?

What could she have done? Did this mean they weren't together anymore?

He shook his head, trying to dislodge the thought. It was none of his business, really. He should recognize it for what it was: the conniving gossip that fueled the FOHs. Nothing more. Yet he just couldn't stop these silly, Technicolor fantasies from rolling through his mind: Gaia beating Jake to a pulp, Gaia suspending him by his Calvin Klein underwear from the school's flagpole, Gaia renouncing him publicly as the most boring mammal on the planet.

Ed really had nothing against Jake. Jake was. . . Jake. He was a decent enough guy. Sure, he looked like he'd just breezed off the set of *The OC,* but he wasn't the ego on legs one would expect. And he did seem to treat Gaia well. Ed couldn't hate him. But he didn't have to like the guy either, right? He didn't wish anything horrible on him—nothing beyond a bad case of acne or a sudden relocation to Addis Ababa—but he was also not going to be Jake Montone's friend, ally, or fan.

Which brought him back to that pesky question at hand: *What the hell did Gaia do to Jake?*

The phone rang. Ed quickly snatched it up, grateful for the opportunity to concentrate on something else. "Ed's room. Ed speaking."

"Hey. How's the convalescing?"

Ed smiled. There was no mistaking Kai's peppy, staccato inflections. "I am so convalesced. Convalesced is I. Any more soup or bed rest and I'll become super-human. Which is why I'm going to school tomorrow."

Kai gasped slightly. "Really? Ed, that's excellent! I wish I could be there."

"What? You aren't going to school?" Ed asked, feeling genuinely disappointed.

"No. Remember? Mom's taking me to check out Hartford College. You know, that all-women's school? There's no way in hell I'll choose that place, but hey, if it means missing calculus, I'll play along."

"I totally understand. Still, you will be missed." Ed sighed. Something told him he might be needing Kai tomorrow. As a friend or maybe a diversion. Kai was one of the few happy, low-stress, low-maintenance things in his life at the moment.

"Aw, that's sweet," Kai murmured. "You know, I'll be thinking of you, too. There're some swanky dress shops in Hartford Mom knows about. I'm going to see what they have in the way of prom wear. How are you doing finding a tux? Did you check out those web sites yet?"

"Yep. Only they weren't much help. Single-breasted versus double-breasted? Ascots versus bow ties? Vests versus cummerbunds? There's more to this tuxedo-renting situation than I previously thought. Yet they all look pretty much the same. What is it, exactly, that distinguishes one black tuxedo from another? Their vintage? Their inner personality?"

"Poor thing," she teased. "You really are lost, aren't you?"

"It's okay. I'm actually thinking about starting my own brand of tux. Something a little less confining. Baggier pants—maybe with a drawstring, even. Matching knit cap. Think of it as skater boi formal wear."

"Go ahead," she said, laughing. "And you can fashion yourself a new date while you're at it."

"Are you kidding me? I'm the perfect date. In fact, I just got an e-mail from Megan Stein about how cool it is you and I going together."

"Really?" Kai sounded suspicious. "I'm surprised she was even interested. Was that all she wanted?"

"Sort of. She also wanted to fill me in on the latest gossip. Something vague about Gaia doing something to Jake." He tried to sound offhand, but for some reason, his voice grew stronger, with an added note of urgency.

There was a slight pause. Then Ed heard the staticky sound of Kai sighing into the receiver. "Yeah. That," she said.

"Do you know what she's talking about?" he asked, casting aside all pretense of indifference.

"Yeah," Kai replied haltingly. "I think so."

"Well. . . ?" Ed clenched his fist around the receiver, trying not to sound irritated. "What did you hear?"

"I ran into Amy van Cline at Starbucks and she said Tammie Deegan had just been in, telling everyone how Gaia cheated on Jake with Skyler Rodke."

"*What*? No way!"

"Hey, I'm just saying what she told me." He could hear it now. There was clearly a hurt tone behind Kai's voice.

"I'm sorry. It's just that it's too weird. Gaia would never do a thing like that."

But even as he said it, a back compartment of his brain was spinning up a whole new line of thought. Why was he so sure Gaia wouldn't cheat? He'd certainly seemed to think she was capable of it when they were dating and she was getting chummy with Sam Moon again. Of course. . . she never did get back together with Sam, like he'd assumed she would. But *Skyler Rodke*? The guy probably had regular facials, for chrissake. How could Gaia be with a guy who probably had five different types of hair gel in his bathroom cabinet?

Besides, the Gaia he'd come to know—as friend, confidant, and soul mate—just wasn't capable of that sort of deception. In fact, the only times he'd known her to be devious, she'd either been in danger or protecting someone. So could this mean she was in trouble? She had been acting really strange lately. Crying, obsessing over non-Gaia things like prom and fashion. What did it all mean?

"I'm sure it's no big deal."

"Huh?" Was that Kai? Oh, yeah. He was talking with Kai. "Sorry. Didn't mean to spaz. I just hate gossip. It's so. . . high school."

"Right." Kai's pitch had fallen several notes. "Well, listen. I really should go. Good luck with tomorrow and your big comeback."

"Thanks. Have fun on your trip. Call me when you get back."

"I will," she replied, rather unenthusiastically. "Bye."

Brilliant going, Fargo, he scolded himself as he hung up the phone. Kai was so great, so easygoing, so undeserving of him. And if he wasn't careful, he was going to completely ruin things with her over this relentless obsession with All Things Gaia.

Which reminded him. . . what the hell was going on between her and Skyler?

GAIA STOOD ON THE LAWN JUST

Tightly Focused Hatred

below her window, gauging her fear. So far there was none. In fact, she felt great. It was nice to slink out of that depressing little hovel for a while (thank you, Jake, for revealing this nifty little escape hatch).

167

A cool breeze wafted over her, tickling her cheeks with the loose wisps of hair around her face. She could smell the breath of the city—salty sea air spiked with gasoline and just a hint of East River sludge. It invigorated her, beckoned to her, calling her forth into the heart of the city.

She decided to walk down the street. After all, standing in the yard wasn't a true test of her panic. Other than Suko or a wayward rat, she wouldn't really find much to fear.

Careful to stay in the shadows, she stole across the lawn and turned onto the sidewalk. Gaia felt an exhilarating rush of freedom. She'd forgotten how in sync she was with the nighttime. Her senses sharpened and her body felt revved. Even her mind seemed squeegeed of the day's emotional residue. She should have been a cat. Or a nighthawk. Some creature no one would ever force into the sun.

Gaia passed by the shuttered shops and sleeping apartment buildings. Couples walked past hand in hand, probably on their way from the theater. A group of noisy men dressed in athletic gear spilled out of a nearby bar and started hailing a cab. She even had to veer around a pair of winos stumbling crookedly down the sidewalk, their bottles, swaddled in brown paper bags, clutched tightly to their chests.

At the other end of the block she paused, checking for fear. But she felt no trepidation whatsoever. In fact, she felt completely at ease, primed for action. Even—dare she say it?—content.

Okay. Maybe she should go just a little farther.

It was time for the ultimate test. Washington Square Park was just a few minutes away. At this hour it would be full of all sorts of things a normal person would find frightening. Just one stroll through the darkest path and she'd know beyond a doubt whether there was any fear left in her system at all.

Soon Gaia saw the familiar arch in the distance. She quickened her pace, her feet knowing instinctively which path to take. It was as if she were coming home from a long voyage, a probe returning to its mother ship.

And there was still no fear.

Instead her body buzzed with expectation—the familiar thrill she always got when bubbly adrenaline coursed through her veins, topping off her power supply. She hurried past the chess tables, through a grove of trees, and into the park's dark, chewy center.

She knew what she wanted—what she almost *needed* to find. The park had never let her down before, and she hoped it wouldn't fail her now.

It didn't. As Gaia made her way past a circle of park benches, she saw a group of people huddled in the trees beyond. It was her old buddies, the Droogs. There were five of them standing menacingly around a pair of twenty-something-year-old girls, circling and cackling like a pack of half-starved hyenas.

"Hey, there," she called out, advancing toward them without hesitation. "Yoo-hoo. I'm ho-o-ome."

This was so worth it, if only to see the confused looks on their crazed chimpanzee faces. After gaping at her, then at each other, they turned away from the scared, shaking girls and ambled toward Gaia.

That's right, she urged silently. *Come to Papa.*

Sensing opportunity, the two girls immediately ran for it. None of the Droogs bothered to follow.

"I don't believe it," said the tallest of the lot, a skinny, pimply-faced monster with four piercings in each eyebrow. "It's *her.*"

Gaia smiled sweetly at them. "You got it. The bitch is back."

A second later they were on her.

It was nothing like the fight outside the boarding-house or the scuffle in the alley next to Skyler's building. Gaia felt no hesitation, no panic whatsoever. Only a tightly focused hatred. She easily dodged their blows and planted her own, as if the entire scene had been expertly choreographed.

An elbow to one's nose and he was on his back, hacking up blood. A jab to another's solar plexus and he immediately fell forward and curled up like a baby. As a third one charged toward her, switchblade in hand, she skillfully stepped out of the way and turned his own momentum against him, sending him crashing into a nearby tree.

How could she have ever found this daunting? She was like a racehorse that had been stabled for far too long. Her limbs and muscles practically sang with pleasure. *This was what she was meant to do. She knew it with every hormonally charged molecule in her being.*

With a high, exhilarating kick she sent another attacker flying backward into one of his buddies. Their heads collided, knocking them senseless.

There was only one left now. The tall goon with the bad skin and eyebrow jewelry. Three others were unconscious and a fourth was sputtering on the ground, clutching his head and seemingly self-destructing. Gaia felt slightly let down. It had all happened too fast.

The guy loomed in front of her, grinning maniacally. He too had a knife—a crude, blunt hunting blade. "I knew you would be back," he said in his high, frenzied voice.

"Is that so?"

"Yeah. God told me." He lunged toward her, arms flailing wildly.

"Oh, please." What was this? A fight or a sermon? *She'd had her fill of religious-sounding street trash.*

With one arm she deflected his attack, knocking the blade from his hand. With the other she hit him hard with an uppercut punch to the lower jaw.

Gaia heard a muffled crunching sound and his

head snapped backward. When he raised it again, his mouth hung slightly askew.

And still he came after her, his hands scrabbling about in front of him, grasping for any part of her. She danced easily out of the way, almost bored with the whole proceeding. At least the guy couldn't talk anymore.

Finally, as he gave another desperate dive, she finished him off with a fast chop to the neck. He crumpled to the ground, moonlight glinting off the metal studs on his face.

Gaia turned in a slow circle, staring down at her handiwork. For a second she felt a surge of satisfaction seeing all the limp, groaning skinheads. Then suddenly her vision blurred. Her body got that heavy, droopy feeling, warning her that her energy supply would soon be depleted.

She managed to make it to the front of the park, to her favorite secluded bench. She dropped onto it and stretched out on the cool wooden planks. This time she didn't fight the darkness.

Just before the lid slammed shut on her consciousness, she wondered if she might wake up freaked and disoriented again, like last time. Somehow, though, she knew she wouldn't.

To: L
From: K
Re: Update

Previous subject located again. Just spotted in WSP fighting with five unknown assailants. Subject's combat skills appear to be at a higher level than last time. Impeccable timing and motor control.

Do you wish monitoring to continue? Please advise.

To: K
From: L
Re: Update

Affirmative. Keep a tail on subject at all times and report periodically. Make note of subject's body language and all individuals she associates with.

Under no circumstances should you share intel with anyone but me.

So old Gaia is back. As the classic blues song goes, "The fear is gone," and so is new, fear-laden Gaia.

I don't know how I feel about it. In a way I'm relieved. I'm free to fight, *really* fight, and protect people I love. I'd thought fear would give me an edge in battle, but it didn't. It only gave me one more person to fight—myself.

I also thought fear would make me more normal. It did make things matter that I typically don't give a damn about. Suddenly I was worried about prom and how I looked and fitting in with the right people—a regular *Seventeen* subscriber. But did it really help my social life? Hardly. The FOHs never truly became friends (although that doesn't seem like such a tragedy now), and I only confused and alienated the people who truly matter to me, like Jake and Ed.

But I can't help wondering if

I could have eventually gotten this fear thing down. Maybe it was just too much, too fast. Unlike normal people, who learn to master fear from birth, I got it dumped on me all at once at the ripe old age of seventeen. I needed time to adapt. It's like I was given a grand piano and after banging around on it, frustrating myself and annoying the neighbors, it gets snatched away from me just when I was sounding out "Chopsticks."

Overall, I just feel robbed. This is the second time in my life I've been promised fear only to have it fail. The first time doesn't really count, though. When Loki injected me with that serum, promising me a normal life, all I got was a long, nightmarish psychotic episode. This time it was real fear—at least, I'm pretty sure it was, having nothing to compare it to. I was Gaia the Meek instead of Gaia the Crazed Lunatic. I was a blubbery, cowardly, self-doubting disaster, but

I was a normal disaster. I still fell within the broad category of natural teenage *Homo sapiens*.

A few years ago I was watching this show on the Discovery Channel about the ascent of our species. At one part in the program it said that our fear allowed us to evolve and survive—prosper, even. When a caveman saw something resembling a saber-toothed tiger coming toward him or stumbled upon a snake shape in the grass, he would run first and grunt questions later. If it weren't for fear, our only contribution to history would have been as human McNuggets for prehistoric carnivores.

So I can't help but wonder, now that I'm fearless again, will I *personally* evolve? Or am I stuck in neutral, doomed to make the same mistakes again and again until I eventually fall prey to something or someone I don't recognize as dangerous?

GAIA DISENTANGLED HERSELF FROM

Excited Sizzle

the rose trellis and slid onto the narrow stone ledge separating Collingwood's first and second stories. All she had to do was sidle along the wall until she reached her half-open window and climb back inside. Easy. Except for one small, irritating-as-hell problem.

She had to pass by Zan's bedroom window to get to her own. And Zan's room, which had been dark when Gaia left, was now filled with light, her window gaping wide.

Gaia inched forward and peered into the room. Sure enough, there was Zan, sitting in the middle of her floor. Across from her sat a thin, hawk-nosed guy with shockingly white skin and equally shocking jet black hair. The two of them were leaned into each other, completely silent, like the tilt before a kiss. Gaia suddenly felt like a high-wire Peeping Tom. Could she possibly slide past without them noticing?

She was just about to tiptoe across, hoping they'd be too into each other to notice her balancing on the ledge like some giant blond pigeon, when something made her look back.

Was it her imagination, or did she see the gleam of something metal between them?

"That was awesome!" the guy exclaimed. "Okay, your turn."

There was a slight flurry of movement and then they were still again. Zan's right hand lifted, her fingers gripping the body of an `open three-inch switchblade`. Gaia watched as Zan slowly inched the jagged point forward. It looked like she was playing airplane with it until Gaia realized she was aiming for something—and judging by the knife's altitude, she was zeroing in on her pal's left eye.

In a fluid, catlike motion Gaia leapt through the open window, grabbed Zan's right wrist, and pulled it straight up.

"What the hell?" she demanded, wrenching the blade from Zan's grasp. "Is gouging out eyeballs all the rage now?"

Zan and the raven-haired guy just laughed.

"Relax, Gaia! It's only a game," Zan said in an eager, twittery tone. "We were just seeing if we could make each other flinch, and we never could!"

"Yeah, man," the guy added in an equally keyed-up voice. "It's so cool! You should try it."

"But you could have really hurt him!"

Zan and her pal exchanged fake-astonished looks and burst out laughing again. "That's the whole point!" Zan cried. "We don't care! Besides, I'm so incredibly focused, there's no way I could hurt him."

Gaia stared at her. Zan's pupils were so dilated, her

eyes appeared black instead of their usual blue. That plus the `excited sizzle` in her voice all pointed to one obvious fact: she was flying on Invince. Her guy friend, too.

But as Gaia peered into her eyes, she noticed something else. Something familiar—the very same thing that had been missing from her own reflection the last time she'd studied it.

She sat on Zan's bed, the knife still tight in her fist. "Hey, Zan? Tell me something. What does it feel like when you're on Invince?"

A glorious, all-out smile conquered Zan's face. "Amazing!" she breathed.

The guy nodded in blissed-out agreement.

"Yeah, but can you describe it? I mean, what exactly does it do to you?"

Zan fell back onto her braided oval rug and gazed beatifically at the ceiling. "It's like. . . I feel completely relaxed, yet powerful, too. Like nothing in the world can scare me."

Gaia raised her eyebrows. "Really? Nothing at all?"

"Not a thing. Never, ever, ever."

Hmmm, Gaia thought. *Interesting. . .*

"Why? You want us to hook you up?"

"No, thanks," she said, standing. She snapped the switchblade shut and tossed it onto the snarl of blankets atop Zan's unmade bed. "I don't think I'll be needing it."

From: dboy@shoalcreek.net
To: gaia13@alloymail.com
Subject: re: Be careful!

Gaia,
Your letter was full of clouds. Glorious Gaia
in the dark city. Don't let the black come in.
Stay in the yellow. Stay in the bright!

Just to be
safe, he kept
his eye on
the teapot,
ready to **normal**
duck in case
abnormalness
it came
hurtling
toward him.

JAKE STOOD OUTSIDE OLIVER'S
apartment and listened as the footsteps grew louder and louder. Soon
he heard the rattling of locks and the
dull clunk of a dead bolt shifting
backward. He held his breath as the
knob turned and the steel door
slowly swung open. He really, really
dreaded this moment.

**Too
Surreal**

"Jake." Oliver stood before him, his deep-set blue
eyes warm and welcoming. Jake could barely meet
them. He didn't deserve their warmth. "Come in. I was
just having some tea. Please, join me." Oliver pulled
the door wider and gestured for him to enter the
apartment.

"Thanks." Jake ambled across the threshold. His
fists were shoved deep in his jacket pockets, making
him shuffle forward as if handcuffed.

Jake took his usual seat in the leather armchair and
gazed up at the pressed-tile ceiling. Meanwhile Oliver
puttered about in the galley kitchen, pouring drinks.
Jake knew the man was just being a considerate host,
but he couldn't help resenting the suspense it created.
He just wanted to get this over with—just take
his licking and get out.

"Here you are." Oliver stood over him, holding a
tray. Jake sat up and watched as Oliver set out two
cups of tea, milk, sugar cubes, spoons, and two small

dishes of *pain au chocolate*. "So, tell me about Gaia," Oliver said offhandedly, carefully spooning sugar into his cup.

Jake marveled at his everyday tone of voice, as if they were just two associates, having tea, chatting about the day's events. He was also grateful he was too occupied to meet Oliver's gaze.

"I saw her," Jake said, beginning with the good news.

Oliver looked up, his spoon pausing in midstir. "You did? When?"

"Tonight. I broke into her room at the boarding-house and hid until she came home." He paused, waiting to see if Oliver would commend him for this ingenious course of action. He didn't. "It was just before curfew when she arrived, and she wasn't very happy to see me."

"What happened? How did she look?"

"Well, that's the thing. She seemed really strange."

"Strange? How?"

"She just. . . wasn't herself. She was really mad at me for hiding out and accused me of not caring about her, saying she never got any of my messages. Then I tried to warn her about Skyler Rodke and she lost it."

Oliver sat far forward, his elbows propped on his knees. "Be more specific, Jake. What did she say exactly?"

"She said I was only trying to play mind games with

her. She said Skyler was wonderful and perfect, and how dare I accuse him of anything bad. Apparently the guy's even taking her to prom." He paused, hanging his head slightly. "Then she broke up with me and threatened to scream for Suko if I didn't leave."

Jake sat miserably for a few minutes, staring at a worn spot on his jeans. At any moment Oliver would unleash his wrath, accuse him of pushing his niece into further danger. He'd say that he regretted ever trusting him and that he and Gaia were both better off with Jake not in their lives. Then he'd dump tea on him and kick him back out onto the street.

But there was nothing but silence. After a moment Jake risked glancing up.

To his utter amazement, Oliver was smiling. He was rubbing his chin in a far-off, thoughtful way as he stared over Jake's shoulder out the window.

Eventually his eyes snapped back onto Jake's. "You've done a good job," he said. "Thank you."

Jake sat there, speechless, wondering if Oliver had misconstrued everything he'd told him. Just to be safe, he kept his eye on the teapot, ready to duck in case it came hurtling toward him. "You—you're not. . . I mean. . . I expected you to be mad."

Oliver smiled. "I too have had emotional run-ins with Gaia. I know how difficult she can be," he said, his voice soothingly sympathetic. "I'm sorry my niece was so harsh with you. But whatever you do, don't give up on her. In spite of everything she said, she still needs you, Jake. Now more than ever."

"All right," Jake mumbled, nodding distractedly. This was `too surreal.` He'd expected anger, disappointment, possibly even tears. Instead Oliver was giving him a medal and sending him back into battle? Obviously his brain was way too feeble to comprehend the workings of this great man's mind.

Oliver stood abruptly, signaling the end of the conversation, and Jake followed suit. "Please keep in touch," Oliver said, clapping him on the back and steering him toward the door. "Keep close tabs on Gaia, and if you see or hear anything unusual—anything at all—contact me immediately."

"All right," Jake said again, his head bobbing in small, circular motions. Oliver clapped him on the back in a good-buddy type of gesture that also managed to propel him back into the corridor.

"Remember what I said," Oliver urged from the doorway. "No matter what, don't give up on her."

"I won't."

"Good. Good night, Jake," he said, and closed the door.

Jake stood in the long, echoey hallway, staring down at the stained concrete floor. *I'll never give up on her, Oliver,* he uttered silently. *But I'm not sure what good it'll do.*

Because Gaia has most definitely given up on me.

I have made a mistake.

It seems I have underestimated this Skyler Rodke. I'm not proud of it. It was a crucial error—possibly even a costly one. But luckily I still have time to rectify it.

You see, I had assumed that Rodke was like other opportunistic thugs. I figured he saw a prize for the taking and took it, using the typically crude tactics a second-rate criminal would use. Namely threats, intimidation, deception, abduction, and primitive physical violence. But now I find this is not the case. Instead he has resorted to such psychological trickery one would expect from. . . well, from me, to be precise.

The boy obviously recognizes what a divine gift Gaia is, and he knows that a prize like that must be handled carefully. He's found her greatest (and possibly only) weakness: her loneliness. And somehow he's already managed to win her confidence.

But there are risks to getting too close to one's prey.

Little does the boy know what he's dealing with. Gaia is mine. We share blood and a common destiny. She has been rebelling against this obvious truth—normal for a teenager—but the facts still remain. I know things about her that he does not. I have connections to her past, present, and future at my disposal. And most of all, I have patience.

This line of attack he's using will soon self-destruct on its own. Because worse than threatening Gaia, worse than abducting her, even worse than attacking her is to gain her trust and then betray her.

And the consequences of that mistake will be something worth waiting for.

THERE IT WAS. STARING HER RIGHT in the face.

Gaia was once again examining her reflection, this time in front of her dresser mirror at the boardinghouse. And this time she saw what had been missing the day before at Skyler's.

Her Own Obi-wan Kenobi

It was an indefinable quality behind the eyes—a sort of deep-set steadiness or unflinching calm. Zan had a version of that look whenever she was flying on Invince. Gaia had recognized it just now in the rock-steady way Zan stared back at her. Never wavering, never pulling back for comfort's sake. Guess it took fearlessness to know fearlessness.

Of course, Gaia's eyes also had that saggy, no-sleep, just-clobbered-a-whole-basketball-team quality to them. She really should get some rest before going to school tomorrow. Otherwise she'd be dead by the time she met up with Skyler.

Skyler. . .

Gaia frowned at her mirror image. She was really spending a lot of time with him lately. Why was that? Sure, he was incredibly nice to her, but was there more to it? Did she truly like the guy? Her image frowned back, unflinching but thoroughly confused.

She turned away and plopped onto the end of her bed. Maybe she could figure it out logically. Let's see. . . . Skyler was kind, good-looking, and incredibly classy. All big pluses. He'd helped her out of half a dozen scrapes, fed her, bathed her, cheered her up, and, not counting that big kiss, never once taken advantage of her. Again all good. So why was she confused about the way she felt for him?

Because it *wasn't* logical. While her rational side ticked off all his good points, her instincts told her something vital was missing. She enjoyed being with Skyler, but it came nowhere near the warmth she felt for Ed, or the flutters she had for Sam, or even the kinship she shared with Jake. And no math in the world could solve that.

All right, then. So why had she had `that grand mal meltdown` with Jake earlier? Why had she practically tossed him out the window for saying Skyler was up to something?

Of course she had been mad at Jake. He'd been a monumental jerk for not calling and for buddying up with her evil, nutcase uncle. But her little drama had more to do with Skyler. It was as if she couldn't stand to hear anything bad about him. From anyone. Ever.

Gaia stretched out on her yellow chenille bedspread and stared at the faint gray stains on the ceiling. She was becoming rather dependent on Skyler. `It was nice, really. Sort of like having her own Obi-wan`

Kenobi. But could it be she was becoming a bit too slobbery and all-consumed by the guy? Why was she fighting to maintain this half-god image of him? And perhaps even more curious—why was he, a gorgeous and magnetic *college* student, for goodness sake, so hell-bent on spending all his free time with her?

Yes. The more she thought of it, the more troubling it became. Was Skyler truly as devoted to her as it seemed, or did he, like so many others before him, just want a piece of her? Did he merely see a part of himself in her as he claimed, or was he taking advantage of her frail condition? There was only one way to find out the answer. Gaia would have to continue behaving as the fearful ball of nerves she'd been, and study his behavior. She couldn't risk reverting back to her old self. Because whatever it was Skyler might have been looking for, Gaia had a hunch he wanted it from Fearful Gaia. Not Fearless Gaia.

A knock sounded and the door swung halfway open. "Gaia? Are you still awake?" Suko stood in the doorway, wearing a red silk housecoat. Her black hair, free of its usual bun, tumbled gracefully about her shoulders, making her look more feminine and beautiful than Gaia had ever seen her.

"Uh, yeah. Sorry. I just had some last-minute studying. I'm turning in right now." She hopped off the bed and began busily peeling back the covers and fluffing pillows.

"Wait, please, Gaia. There is something I wish to speak to you about."

Uh-oh. Did she know she'd snuck out? Had she seen her little trapeze act outside? "Sure. What is it?"

"It is about this. . . friend of yours. The tall, dark-haired one. Jake is his name?"

"Yeah. That's right. Jake." Again uh-oh. Did she know Jake had been in her room that evening?

"Could you please tell him not to call and come by so many times?"

Gaia's eyes widened. "What do you mean? When did he do all this?"

"He called many times and he came by at least twice this weekend. This morning after you left and also yesterday afternoon. I saw him on the porch, talking with Zan. Did she not tell you?"

"No. But. . . I haven't really spoken with her much this weekend."

"He seemed quite upset to find you gone. He could not understand why you did not answer his messages on your cell phone."

Gaia scowled at the floor. *So he was telling the truth? He really did check up on me?* Something must be wrong with her phone. Either that or—

"Gaia?"

She glanced back up at Suko. "Yes?"

"Tell him please to not bother us so much. And

please try to keep people informed of your where-abouts. I am not a secretary for you girls."

"Right. Sorry."

Suko nodded appreciatively and then quietly shut the door. Gaia could barely hear her soft footsteps padding back to her room.

Gaia felt oddly disoriented, as if everything in the world had been yanked three feet to the left. Her fear had completely vanished—she was back to her **normal abnormalness**. But for some reason, nothing else seemed the same.

I have never been what you'd call religious. In fact, I was often criticized for being somewhat flippant about the whole supreme deity hard sell.

Once when we were kids, Aunt Agatha took me, Chris, and Liz to her Evangel Temple. We sat in the back and watched as a man stood in front of the assembled congregation, ranting and shouting and shaking this large black Bible. After a while people started getting really worked up. Some cried. Some yelled out hallelujahs. And quite a few of them closed their eyes and lifted up their arms. Chris leaned over to me and said, "How come they have their hands up like that?" and I whispered, "Better reception."

Aunt Agatha sent us out to the car for disturbing God with our giggling.

Lately, I have to say, I've been feeling almost religious about my life. Things are going so beautifully with Gaia, all

according to plan. I've managed
to discredit her lunkhead
boyfriend and her stupid, petty
friends. I even have her starting
to doubt her own father—plenty of
time to finish that up while he's
away saving the world.

Before long I'll have her completely dependent on me. She
won't know what to think or eat
or even when to breathe without
consulting with me first. And the
beauty of it is, she'll never
even consider crossing me,
because to do so would make her
utterly helpless.

Eventually she'll be pro-
grammed to respond to me and me
alone. And once someone thinks of
you as their salvation, nothing
will tear them away. Think of a
mighty stallion. Even he won't
run from his stable when it's on
fire.

There's something intrinsi-
cally mythic about this whole
thing. It's even evident in our
names. She is Gaia, which means
the earth, and I am Skyler, the

heavens. She is raw, chaotic power and I am her conduit. Together we are a combined force of nature too intense for regular society.

I can't help but think there's some divine destiny at work here. As if my brilliant plan is only a subset of a larger, celestial scheme—something grander than even I can imagine. Could my coming together with Gaia have been scripted by our Lord?

Gaia is mine. More than that, Gaia is me. Raise up your arms and feel our power. Amen.

It was like she'd fallen into a classic horror **carnival**— story. Everywhere she **like** went, she was haunted by the **vibe** ghosts of boyfriends past.

OF COURSE JAKE WOULD BE THE

Irrational Extremist

first person Gaia spied when she entered school the next morning. It was par for the course in the whole ironic game of life. You forget your umbrella, so a thunderstorm hits as you walk home. You get in the fast-moving grocery line, so some little old lady in front of you tries to pay with pennies. You try to avoid someone you're feeling monumentally confused about, so you end up nose to nose with them the minute you enter neutral territory.

She should have expected it. After all, she couldn't exactly dive into broom closets all day whenever he came near. But what she could never have prepared herself for was how utterly pitiful he looked.

Seeing him there, leaning against the obnoxious tile mosaic of the school seal, she was instantly reminded of those wax figures in Madame Tussauds. His skin was so sickly pale, it seemed almost translucent. His dark tresses looked sadly wilted. And each eye had a dark crevice beneath it, as if someone had forcibly pushed the eyeballs farther back into their sockets.

But more than that, there was just so little life emanating from him. He hardly moved, and he barely seemed to notice his surroundings. It was as if he'd been propped carelessly against the wall and forgotten about. If he hadn't straightened up the moment he saw her, she probably would have gone over and taken his pulse.

"Hey," he said, walking toward her.

Gaia hesitated slightly, then adjusted her trajectory to meet him. "Hey," she said back, her eyes instinctively searching for a broom closet.

She really hoped he wouldn't rope her into a conversation about her weekend hysterics. How could she enlighten him any if she still couldn't fathom it all herself?

"I was just wondering," he began, looking even more cramped and uncomfortable than she felt. "Are you all right?"

She raised her eyebrows. *He* was asking if *she* was all right? He was the one who looked like he'd slept in a train station—if he'd slept at all. "I'm fine. Thanks."

"Good." He paused, running his hand through his sagging forelock. "Listen, uh. . . I'm sorry about surprising you last night. I shouldn't have hidden out like that."

"It's okay," she said, shrugging.

The relief in his eyes was almost too much to bear. For a moment she considered offering her own apology for having wigged out on him so horribly and uncontrollably. She could blame it on too much coffee or a period from hell.

But then she reminded herself that this was the

same guy who'd gotten all nicey-nice with Loki. The guy who refused to believe her warnings and completely discounted her feelings. *So*, she thought, *let him stew a little*.

Besides, she was still sorting it all out herself. She had no idea why her fearlessness had returned or why she kept having encounters with Droogs or why she turned into an `irrational extremist` whenever someone dissed Skyler. If this had anything at all to do with Loki, it would probably be best to avoid Jake altogether—at least until she figured out what was going on.

"So . . you want to meet after school and talk somewhere?" Jake asked, hope stirring behind his sunken eyes.

"I can't. I have plans."

"With who? Skyler?" His voice took on a rough, growling quality.

She didn't answer.

"Gaia, you have to tell me what's going on between you two. I deserve to know what's happening!"

"I have to go to class." She turned and headed toward a nearby stable of lockers. It pained her to behave so brutally toward him. Of course he deserved to know what was going on between Skyler and her. But she had to continue on as if nothing had changed in the last twenty-four hours—including her feelings of anger toward Jake. Until she had a better grasp of things. A better understanding of why exactly she was spending so much time with Skyler. And in order to get the information she was after, she'd have to act exactly the way she acted when she had fear. So that no one's suspicions would be raised. Even if it meant breaking Jake's heart.

"Wait." Jake grabbed her arm, his pitch softer, more conciliatory. "I'm sorry. Can we please just talk some more?"

"I don't think so," she said, wrenching out of his grasp.

"Please, just hear me out," he pleaded. "Can you just listen to my concerns for one freaking minute?"

She eyed him suspiciously, stepping slowly backward as if wanting a more complete view. His eyes were wild and worried looking. Red blotches had erupted across his pale skin. Somehow she'd done this to him.

Did everyone eventually freak out on her? There was Oliver, and there was Loki. Natasha the mother figure and Natasha the diabolical traitor. Skyler and Scary Skyler. Again Gaia felt oddly misplaced in her own life, as if she were seeing everything through a distorted fun house mirror.

"This is important, Gaia," he continued begging her. "I'm trying to help you."

No. She had to raise shields, shut down, switch to sleeper mode. She spun around and continued walking away from Jake.

"Come back!" he shouted. "Don't meet him after school, Gaia! Please don't!"

But the desperation in his voice only made her speed away faster.

OF ALL PLACES, HE SAW HER IN

Joy and Surprise

the library. Ed had shuffled in before school, needing to pick up a pile of catch-up assignments, and there she was. Gaia stood out like a supermodel among the typical denizens of the library— bespectacled bookworms and sallow-faced computer fanatics. She stood in a corner of the literature section, leaning against a shelf and thumbing through some gilded hardback. What could she be doing there?

Should he approach her? Ed stood scuffing his tennis shoes against the charcoal-colored industrial carpeting. His entire body said yes, except for the one tiny alcove in his mind, which seemed to have power over his legs.

On the one hand, it was the perfect time and place. Nice and private. And enough time had passed since their last meeting for it to feel proper again. Yet the way she huddled in the corner seemed to suggest that she really didn't want to be approached right now.

He was just about to turn away when she glanced up at him. "Ed!" Her face filled with joy and surprise. "Jesus Christ! When did you get out of the hospital?" She rushed toward him.

Ed stood stock still, watching her advance. For one gleeful second he wondered if she might actually embrace him. But suddenly her momentum tapered off. She stopped a half a foot away from him and hugged the book to her chest. Ed glanced at the title on the cover. Kafka's *Metamorphosis*.

"A couple of days ago," he replied. "My parents didn't want me to come to school today, but I managed to convince them. You know me. Always the responsible student."

She smiled. "I'm glad you're better."

"Me too. I'm glad I'm better, too." He smiled back at her, nodding. *See?* he told himself. *This is nice. This is natural.* He continued nodding and smiling. Seconds passed. Suddenly it wasn't feeling so natural anymore.

"So. . . . uh. . ." He searched his mind for something to say and alighted upon the question that had been nagging him for the past twenty-four hours. "I got this weird e-mail from Megan yesterday. Did, um. . . did something happen between you and Skyler Rodke?" He laughed nervously. "The way the girls are talking, it's like the scandal of the century."

He stared at her intently. He was giving her a way out, a chance to explain.

Something shifted behind Gaia's eyes, shuttering out all depth and emotion. "Yeah, well. Gotta give Megan something to live for, you know?"

Ed laughed politely, making mental note of the fact that she didn't deny anything. It had been none of his business, really. He knew that. But it just didn't sound like the Gaia he knew. He couldn't help feeling worried.

"Anyway, I'm really glad you're back," Gaia said over her shoulder. She was leaving now, walking speedily toward the library's double doors. "Take care of yourself, Ed."

"Thanks. You too," he called. But she was already gone.

Ed was left waving at a swinging wooden door and the scattering of energy molecules left in her wake.

Waste of Energy

GAIA SMACKED THE SIDE OF THE vending machine, and her stuck Baby Ruth bar finally plummeted. She reached in and retrieved it, ripping off the top edge of the wrapper.

Not exactly the healthiest of lunch choices, but there was no way Gaia was setting foot in the cafeteria today.

It wasn't the snide whisperings she was avoiding. News of her supposed tryst with Skyler had already spread like the Ebola virus, and people everywhere were shooting smug or snide glances her way. Just a few days ago something like this would have completely crushed her. Now she thought it was amusing. People were always so eager to hear the sordid details of someone's life—as if it were a gripping morality play staged just for them. Maybe if they read more Kafka or Tolstoy, they wouldn't be that way.

Let them talk. She didn't care. The only person she wanted to avoid was Jake. And maybe Ed, with his sad, probing stare. It was like she'd fallen into a classic horror story. Everywhere she went, she was haunted by the ghosts of boyfriends past.

She was confused enough as it was. She didn't need to take on their demands (loud or subtle) to explain her behavior.

"Oh my God, Tammie. Look!" came a familiar screeching voice.

"What?"

"Over *there*," continued the screecher irritably. "I didn't know they let *prostitutes* into the student center."

Gaia almost smiled. Here they came, a gaggle of

FOHs with Megan in the lead. After a long weekend's work of gossip and slander, they were coming to collect their booty, to see her squirm in shame and humiliation.

They were expecting fearful Gaia. Fearful Gaia would cower and tremble and turn various colors. She was no longer fearful Gaia, but she would do her best to offer up a reward.

She tried to look meek as she watched them saunter toward her.

"I'm surprised to see her here," Megan said loudly. "Aren't you guys?"

Her pals agreed in unison, like doo-wop girls in Donna Karan clothes.

"I figured she'd be with her boyfriend."

"Which one?" Tina asked, smirking.

"Right," Megan said, dramatically clapping a hand to her cheek. She turned toward Gaia. "How *do* you keep track?"

Gaia pretended to look stricken. "It's none of your business," she said, her voice weak and whiny. "Why don't you just leave me alone?"

For a moment they just stood there, reveling in their power. Then Megan placed her hands on her hips, cocking them sideways. "Everyone's talking about you, you know," she declared triumphantly.

"Yeah. They can't believe what you did to poor Jake," Tina went on. "The whole school knows the way you dumped him for Skyler. Have you seen him? He's, like, a total wreck. It must be so embarrassing for him."

"Gee, and I wonder how the whole school happened to hear this embarrassing story?" Gaia muttered, anger suddenly flaring inside her. She couldn't believe they had the nerve to act all high and mighty with her when they'd put the whole rumor mill in motion.

"What?" Tammie asked. "What did you say?"

For a moment she saw it. A slight wariness in their eyes. Was Skyler right? Were these girls truly intimidated by her? Was that why they had to butt into her life and stir up all these extra dramatics (as if she needed them)?

But she couldn't stop to ponder that. She had to make these girls think they had power over her. News of Gaia regaining a spine could spoil everything.

She quickly fashioned what she hoped was a hurt, shamed expression on her face and stared down at her scuffed tennis shoes. "Nothing," she mumbled.

Megan leaned forward and lowered her voice to gossip level. "Yes. That's what you are—nothing. And don't forget it." Holding her nose at a regal angle, she turned and walked away, the rest of the girls following like well-dressed ducklings.

Gaia waited a few beats until she was sure they were gone. Then she calmly strode down the corridor, taking a bite of her chocolaty lunch. Christ, how could she have ever cared what those bitches thought of her? What a total **waste of energy.**

She was midway down the hall when she suddenly heard a high, hissing noise, like a puff of escaped steam. "*Psst! Psst!* Gaia!" She turned and saw Liz and Chris standing in front of a row of lockers.

"Gaia! Come here," Liz was calling, beckoning with her hand. Chris, meanwhile, was leisurely shoving books in and out of his locker, not even looking at her.

Gaia veered left and walked toward them. She gave a sloppy wave in greeting, her mouth still full of candy bar.

"What happened this weekend? Is it true you were with Skyler?"

Gaia sighed in exasperation. *Et tu,* Liz? Would she have to give the entire Village School a satisfactory account of her whereabouts over the weekend?

She swallowed her candy. "I was there," she replied. No need to keep it from them. They'd find out anyway.

Liz's eyes widened. "You know, Jake came by our place practically demanding I give him Skyler's address. But I wouldn't. Skyler would have killed me. Besides, I felt I should, you know, look out for you, too."

"Thanks," Gaia mumbled. Chris continued meticulously rearranging his locker, looking like he wanted to be anywhere else.

"So." Liz smiled secretively. "What's going on between you and my brother?"

Gaia met her gaze, sensing her desire to bond, sisterlike, on the issue. But what could she tell her? She didn't really know what was going on. Lately her feelings for Skyler had been incredibly strong and spellbinding but `completely uncategorical`.

"Actually," she began, "I don't know. We're just. . . looking out for each other."

Liz lifted an eyebrow conspiratorially. "Oh, is that what we're calling it? 'Looking out for each other'? Fine. I'll play along." Just then a high-pitched beeping emanated from her pager. "Damn!" she said suddenly, staring down at her pavé-encrusted Bulova watch. "I forgot I have to make up a quiz in English." She shouldered her messenger bag and pivoted toward the north wing of the building. "Let's talk cryptically about this later, then. Okay?" she said with a wry grin. Then, with a toss of her glossy hair and rustle of her silk jacket, she turned and raced down the hall.

Gaia turned to Chris, who was finally gazing at her. Great, now it was his turn to third degree her. "Listen," she said before he could start demanding information. "I'm sorry, but I just don't want to talk about it, okay?"

"That's okay," he said with a shrug. "But just promise me something, all right?" He shut his locker and faced her head-on. "Promise me you'll be really careful."

Gaia was alarmed to see real anxiety in his eyes. What was this about? Chris was typically so unconcerned and cocksure about everything.

"Yeah," she replied. "All right."

He gave her a solemn nod and then strode away after his sister.

Once again Gaia sensed a definite `carnival-like vibe` in the air. Welcome to the fun house. Next stop, the emotional roller coaster.

. . . . people
would be

unflinching

saying she'd
eye
had sex with
Skyler
contact
right in
front of the
building.

GAIA STEPPED OUT OF THE SCHOOL'S

King front entrance, shielding her hand against the outrageously bright sunshine. Students all around her flounced merrily down the steps, drunk with the newfound energy that only a release bell could bring.

She saw him sitting on a stoop across the street. Skyler's platinum blond hair shone like a beacon in the brilliant light.

He saw her and immediately stood up. "Gaia!" he called, raising his right arm as he hailed.

A hundred eyes watched her as she waited to cross the busy street. She could feel them glomming onto her, like tiny invisible leeches, greedily feeding their curiosity.

"Hey," she greeted as she strode up beside him.

"Did you have a nice day at school, sweetheart?" he asked dryly.

"Yes, honey," she played along.

Skyler seemed unaware of their audience. Either that or he was used to being gaped at by the masses.

"Got something for you." He turned and grabbed two Starbucks cups off the low wall of the stoop, holding one out for her. "Milk and two sugars, right?"

She grinned. "Yep, that's it. You know all my secrets."

He smiled proudly.

A few nearby students were now blatantly staring

and whispering. Gaia could only imagine the next day's headlines. By the time the story filtered down the rank assembly lines of the Village School Gossip Factory, people would be saying she'd had sex with Skyler right in front of the building.

"Come on," he said, finally noticing the onlookers. "Let's walk to the park."

Cradling her coffee, Gaia matched his now-familiar leisurely pace along the sidewalk. Soon their spectators were far behind.

"You know," he said as they turned the corner, "I'm a little mad at you."

"You are?" she asked, her brain whirring frantically. What did she do? Had he seen Jake leave her bedroom? Did he hear about her fight in the park?

"You wore your hair up."

Gaia patted the back of her head, fingering her oval tortoiseshell clip. She'd haphazardly shoved some particularly wayward strands in it that morning, forgetting all about Skyler's preference. "Oh. Sorry."

"Forget it. I was just—"

A loud, piercing wail suddenly drowned out Skyler's voice. An ambulance was backing out of a nearby depot, its lights on and siren blaring. It didn't scare Gaia at all. But a startled Skyler jerked backward, reminding Gaia that she needed to put on a show of fear. So she quickly wrenched Skyler's arm and buried her face in his jacket.

"You all right?" he said as the shrill notes of the siren died away in the distance.

She glanced up, smiling sheepishly. "Guess I wigged out a bit. It was just so loud." She released her grip on his jacket and patted his arm lightly. "Did I hurt you?"

"No," he said, laughing. "Come on. Let's cross."

The park lay before them, full of joggers and stroller-pushing urban moms. She and Skyler walked across the street and in through the brick-walled entrance.

Skyler led the way to an empty concrete bench and sat down, his long arms resting regally across the back. Gaia settled in beside him, taking the last, long sip of her coffee.

"I've got a lot planned for us tonight," Skyler said, absently watching the park activities like a king surveying his kingdom.

"Oh?"

"You'll love it." He turned to face her. "You should probably call Suko and give her an excuse for coming home late or maybe not at all. Then we might want to stop by my apartment and freshen up first. This restaurant I'm taking you to is really hard to get into, but I know the code. I got us a reservation for seven-thirty. . . ."

Gaia nodded along as he talked, focusing on the thin rims of gold around his pupils. It was mesmerizing—as if the shadows of tiny moons had moved in front of the solar-powered orbs of his eyes.

Just then she remembered something. She was doing it again. That resolute stare. The `unflinching eye contact.`

Quickly, before he had the chance to notice, she pulled her gaze from his eyes and looked submissively at the ground in front of his feet.

If nothing else, she now had the fear thing down.

the
nine
lives
of
chloe
king

The Fallen

by
CELIA THOMSON

One

As soon as she opened her eyes that morning, Chloe decided that she would go to Coit Tower instead of Parker S. Shannon High, her usual destination on a Tuesday.

She was turning sixteen in less than twenty-four hours, with no real celebration in sight: Paul spent Wednesdays at his dad's house in Oakland, and—far worse—her mom had said something about "maybe going to a nice restaurant." What was a "nice" restaurant, anyway? A place where they served blowfish and foie gras? Where the wine list was thicker than her American civilization textbook? No, thank you.

If Mom found out about the Coit Tower expedition, Chloe would be grounded, completely eliminating any possibility of dinner out. Then Chloe would have a *right* to feel miserable on her sixteenth birthday, at home, alone, punished. The idea was strangely alluring.

She called Amy.

"Hey, want to go to the tower today instead of physics?"

"Absolutely." There was no hesitation, no pause—no grogginess, in fact. For all of Amy's rebel post-punk posturing, Chloe's best friend was a morning person. How did she deal with the 2 A.M. poetry readings? "I'll see you there at ten. I'll bring bagels if you bring the crack."

By "crack" Amy meant Café Eland's distinctive twenty-ounce coffee, which was brewed with caffeinated water.

"You're on."

"You want me to call Paul?"

That was strange. Amy never volunteered to do anything, much less help with group planning.

"Nah, let me guilt him into it."

"Your funeral. See ya."

She dragged herself out of bed, wrapping the comforter around her. Like almost everything in the room, it was from Ikea. Her mom's taste ran toward orange, turquoise, abstract kokopelli statuettes, and blocks of sandstone—none of which fit in a crappy middle-class San Francisco ranch. And since Pateena Vintage Clothing paid a whopping five-fifty an hour, Chloe's design budget was limited. Scandinavian blocks of color and furniture with unpronounceable names would have to do for now. *Anything* beat New Southwest.

She stood in front of the closet, wearing a short pair of boxers and a tank. Chloe was finally developing a waist, as if her belly had been squeezed up to her breasts and down to her butt. Hot or not, it wasn't as though any of it really mattered: her mom grounded her if she so much as even *mentioned* a boy other than Paul.

She threw herself in front of the computer with a wide yawn and jiggled the mouse. Unless Paul was asleep or dead, he could pretty much be located at his computer twenty-four/seven. Bingo—his name popped up in bold on her buddy list.

Chloe: Ame and me are going to Coit Tower today. Wanna come?

Paul: [long pause]

Chloe: ?

Paul: You're not gonna guilt me into it 'cause I'm not gonna be around for your birthday, right?

Chloe: :)

Paul: *groan* ok I'll tell Wiggins I got a National Honor Society field trip or something.

Chloe: ILU, PAUL!!!

Paul: Yeahyeah. Cul8r.

Chloe grinned. Maybe her birthday wasn't going to suck after all.

She looked out the window—yup, fog. In a city of fog, Inner Sunset was the foggiest part of San Francisco. Amy loved it because it was all spooky and mysterious and reminded her of England (although she had never been there). But Chloe was depressed by the damp and cheerless mornings, evenings, and afternoons and liked to flee to higher, sunnier ground—like Coit Tower—at every opportunity.

She decided to play it safe and dressed as if for school, in jeans and a tee and a jean jacket from Pateena's that was authentic eighties. It even had a verse of a Styx song penned carefully in ballpoint on one of the sleeves. She emptied her messenger bag of her textbooks and hid them under her bed. Then she stumbled downstairs, trying to emulate her usual tired-grumpy-morning-Chloe routine.

"You're down early," her mother said suspiciously.

Uneager to pick a fight this morning, Chloe swallowed her sigh. *Every*thing she did out of the ordinary since she'd turned twelve was greeted with suspicion. The first time she'd gotten a short haircut—paid for with her *own* money, thank you very much—her mother had demanded to know if she was a lesbian.

"I'm meeting Ame at the Beanery first," Chloe responded as politely as she could, grabbing an orange out of the fridge.

"I don't want to sound old-fashioned, but—"

"It's gonna stunt my growth?"

"It's a gateway drug." Mrs. King put her hands on her hips. In black Donna Karan capris with a silk-and-wool scoop neck and her pixie haircut, Chloe's mom didn't look like a mom. She looked like someone out of a Chardonnay ad.

"You have *got* to be kidding me," Chloe couldn't keep herself from saying.

"There's an article in the *Week*." Her mother's gray eyes narrowed, her expertly lined lips pursed. "Coffee leads to cigarettes leads to cocaine and crystal methamphetamines."

"Crystal *meth*, Mom. It's crystal *meth*." Chloe kissed her on the cheek as she walked past her to the door.

"I'm talking to you about not smoking, just like the ads say to!"

"Message received!" Chloe called back, waving without turning around.

She walked down to Irving Street, then continued walking north to the southern side of Golden Gate Park, stopping at Café Eland for the two promised coffees. Paul didn't partake; she got him a diet Coke instead. Amy was already at the bus stop, juggling a bag of bagels, her army pack, and a cell phone.

"You know, real punks don't—" Chloe put her hand to her ear and shook it, mimicking a phone.

"Bite me." Amy put down her bag and threw her phone in, pretending not to care about it. Today she wore a short plaid kiltlike skirt, a black turtleneck, fishnets, and cat-eye glasses; the overall effect was somewhere between rebellious librarian and geek-punk.

The two of them were comfortably silent on the bus, just drinking coffee and glad to have a seat. Amy might be a morning person, but Chloe needed at least another hour before she would be truly sociable. Her best friend had learned that years ago and politely accommodated her.

There wasn't much to look at out the bus window; just another black-and-white-and-gray early morning in San Francisco, full of grumpy-faced people going to work and bums finding their street corners. Chloe's reflection in the dusty window was almost monochromatic except for her light hazel eyes. They glowed almost orange in the light when the bus got to Kearny Street and the sun broke through.

Chloe felt her spirits rise: this was the San Francisco of postcards and dreams, a city of ocean and sky and sun. It really was glorious.

Paul was already there, sitting on the steps of the tower, reading a comic book.

"Happy pre-birthday, Chlo," he said, getting up and lightly kissing her on the cheek, a surprisingly mature, touchy-feely act. He held out a brown bag.

Chloe smiled curiously and then opened it—a plastic bottle of Popov vodka was nestled within.

"Hey, I figure if we're going to be truants, why not go all the way?" He grinned, his eyes squeezing into slits zipped shut by his lashes. There was a slight indentation in his short, black, and overgelled hair where his earphones had rested.

"Thanks, Paul." She pointed up. "Shall we?"

"What if you had to choose just one of these views to look at for the rest of your life," Chloe said. "Which one would it be?"

Amy and Paul looked up from each other, almost intrigued. The three of them had been sitting around for the past hour, not really doing much, with Chloe's two best friends occasionally exchanging giggly glances. That had grown old real fast.

Half of Coit Tower's windows showed spectacular, sun-drenched San Francisco scenery, the other nine looked out into a formless, gray-white abyss.

"I'd wait until the sun cleared before making my choice," Amy said, pragmatic as ever. She swirled her cup of coffee for emphasis, mixing its contents. Chloe sighed; she should have expected that answer.

Paul walked from window to window, game. "Well, the bridge is beautiful, with all the fog and clouds and sunset and dawn—"

"Bor-ing," Amy cut in.

"The Transamerica Pyramid is too sharp and weird—"

"And *phallic*."

"I guess I would choose the harbor," Paul decided. Looking over his shoulder, Chloe could see colorful little sailboats coming and going with the wind, dreamy, hazy islands in the distance. She smiled. It was a *very* Paul choice.

"Definitely *not* Russian Hill," Amy added, trying to regain control of the conversation. "Fugly sprawl with a capital *Fug*."

"Made your decision just in time, Paul . . ."

As they watched, low clouds came rolling down from

the hills, replacing each of the nine windows, enclosing the views in a white, total darkness. What should have been a beautiful blue day with puffy white clouds now that they were out of Inner Sunset had rapidly given way to the same old stupid weather.

This wasn't exactly what Chloe had expected for her sixteenth-birthday-school-blow-off day.

To be fair, she always expected more than life was likely to give: in this case, a golden sunny *Stand by Me/Ferris Bueller* these-are-the-best-days-of-our-lives sort of experience.

"So dude," Amy said, changing the subject. "What's up with you and Comrade Ilychovich?"

Chloe sighed and sank down against the wall, taking a last swallow from her own cup. Like Amy's, it was spiked with Paul's birthday present to her. Paul had already drunk his diet Coke and was now sipping directly from the amazingly cheesy plastic vodka flask. Chloe looked dreamily at the black-and-red onion domes on the label.

"He's . . . just . . . so . . . *hot*."

"And *so* out of your league," Amy pointed out.

"Alyec is steely-eyed, chisel-faced young Russian," Paul said with a thick cold war accent. "Possibly with modeling contract. Sources say Agent Keira Hendelson getting close to his . . . *cover*."

"Screw her." Chloe threw her empty cup at the wall, picturing it smashing into the student council's blond little president.

"You *could* be related, you know," Amy pointed out. "That could be a problem. He could be a cousin or nephew or something of your biological parents."

"The old Soviet Union's a big place. Genetically, I think we're okay. It's the getting to actually *date* him that's the problem."

"You could just, I don't know, go up to him and like, *talk* to him or something," Paul suggested.

"He's always surrounded by the Blond One and her Gang of Four," Chloe reminded him.

"Nothing ventured, nothing lost."

Yeah, right. Like *he* had ever asked anyone out.

Amy swigged the last of her coffee and belched. "Oh, crap, I've got to pee."

Paul blushed. He always got nervous when either Amy or Chloe discussed anything like bodily functions in front of him—so usually Chloe didn't talk about that stuff when he was around.

But today she felt . . . well, odd. Jumpy, impatient. Not to mention a little annoyed with both him *and* Amy. This was supposed to be *her* birthday thing. So far it sucked.

"Too bad you can't do it standing up, like Paul," she said, watching him blush out of the corner of her eye. "You could go over the edge."

Now, what had made her say that?

She stood up. Leaning against the stone wall, Chloe peered down. All she could see was swirling whiteness and, off to her left, one water-stained red pylon of the Golden Gate Bridge.

What would happen if I dropped a penny from up here? Chloe wondered. *Would it make a tunnel through the fog? That would be cool.* A tunnel two hundred feet long and half an inch across.

She climbed up into a window and dug into her jeans pocket, hunting for spare change, not bothering to put her other hand on the wall for balance.

The tower suddenly seemed to tilt forward.

"What—," she began to say.

Chloe tried to resteady herself by leaning back into the window frame, grasping for the wall, but the fog had left it clammy and slick. She pitched forward, her left foot slipping out from beneath her.

"Chloe!"

She threw her arms back, desperately trying to rebalance herself. For a brief second she felt Paul's warm fingers against her own. She looked into his face—a smile of relief broke across it, pink flushed across the tops of his high cheekbones. But then the moment was over: Amy was shrieking and Chloe felt nothing catch her as she slipped out of Paul's grasp. She was falling—*falling*—out of the window and off the tower.

This is not happening, Chloe thought. *This is not the way I end.*

She heard the already-muffled screams of her friends

getting fainter, farther and farther away. Something would save her, right?

Her head hit last.

The pain was unbearable, bone crushing and nauseating—the sharp shards of a hundred needles being forced through her as her body compacted itself on the ground.

Everything went black, and Chloe waited to die.

Two

She was surrounded by darkness.

Strange noises, padding footsteps, and the occasional scream echoed and died in strange ways, like she was in a vast cavern riddled with tunnels and caves. Somewhere ahead and far below her, like she was standing at the edge of a cliff, was an indistinct halo of hazy light. It rippled unpleasantly. She started to back away from it. Then something growled behind her and shoved her hard.

Chloe pitched forward toward the light and into empty space.

This was it. This was *death*.

"Chloe? *Chloe?*"

That was odd. God sounded kind of annoying. Kind of whiny.

"Oh my God, she's—"

"Call 911!"

"There's no way she could have survived that fall—"

"GET OUT OF MY WAY!"

Chloe felt like she was spinning, her weight being forced back into her skin.

"You *stupid shithead*!"

That was Amy. That was *definitely* Amy.

"We should call her mom. . . ."

"What do we say? That Chloe is . . . that Chloe's *dead*?"

"Don't say that! It's not true!"

Chloe opened her eyes.

"Oh my God—Chloe . . . ?"

Paul and Amy were leaning over her. Tears and streaky lightning bolts of black makeup ran down Amy's cheeks, and her light blue eyes were wide and rimmed with red.

"You're a-alive?" Paul asked, face white with awe. "There's no way you could have—" He put a hand behind her head, feeling her neck and skull. When he pulled it back, there was only a little blood on his finger.

"You—you didn't—oh my God, it's . . . a . . . miracle . . . ," Amy said slowly.

"Can you move?" Paul asked quietly.

Chloe sat up. It was the hardest thing she could ever remember doing, like pushing herself through a million pounds of dirt. Her head swam, and for a moment there was two of everything, four flat gingerbread friends in front of her. She coughed, then began puking. She tried to lean to the side but couldn't control her body.

After she finished heaving, Chloe noticed that Paul

and Amy were touching her, holding her shoulders. She could just barely feel their hands; sensation slowly crept back over her skin.

"You *should* be dead," said Paul. "There is no. Way. You could have survived that fall."

She was struck by what he said; it seemed true. Yet here she was, alive. Just like that. Why was she so unsurprised?

FEARLESS™

THE END OF AN ERA IS NEAR. . . .
BE AFRAID.

You've watched Gaia break legs.

You've watched her get her heart broken.

But you've never seen her
break free quite like this.

Gaia's high school days are numbered. And
once they've run out, Gaia will make her
most dangerous choice yet.

DON'T MISS THESE LAST ADVENTURES
IN THE BEST-SELLING SERIES:

As many as 1 in 3 Americans
who have HIV... don't know it.

TAKE CONTROL.
KNOW YOUR STATUS.
GET TESTED.

To learn more about HIV testing,
or get a free guide to HIV and
other sexually transmitted diseases:

www.knowhivaids.org
1-866-344-KNOW